John Hearne's Short Fiction

John Hearne, circa 1955

JOHN HEARNE'S
Short Fiction

EDITED BY **SHIVAUN HEARNE**

INTRODUCTION BY **KIM ROBINSON-WALCOTT**

FOREWORD BY **MARLON JAMES**

THE UNIVERSITY OF THE WEST INDIES PRESS
Jamaica • Barbados • Trinidad and Tobago

The University of the West Indies Press
7A Gibraltar Hall Road, Mona
Kingston 7, Jamaica
www.uwipress.com

A catalogue record of this book is available from the
National Library of Jamaica.

ISBN: 978-976-640-606-6 (print)
978-976-640-607-3 (Kindle)
978-976-640-608-0 (ePub)

Cover illustration: Ralph Campbell, untitled (a view of Constant Spring Road,
Kingston, Jamaica, c.1950). Private collection.
Cover and book design by Robert Harris
Set in Bembo 11/15 x 27
Printed in the United States of America

Contents

Foreword

MARLON JAMES

*E*very future writer, at least every one I have met, enters a creative writing class with some set ideas. Not about about what kind of writer he wants to be, but what he already is. That extends to what kind of book he prefers to read, what kind of book he wants to write, what prose he particularly dislikes, and even what constitutes a perfectly creative sentence. Every beginning writer is of course wrong, and sometimes the difference between an illustrious career and an ignominious one is how soon he encounters that person with enough creative and intellectual certitude to tell him that what he has on paper is, beyond a doubt, crap.

This former was me, the latter John Hearne. And that lesson, funnily enough, came not at the beginning of the term, but somewhere midway, when after workshop after workshop of mostly compliments, I showed John Hearne how badly I could misread the best thing he had said about my work. First, some backtracking. I walked into Hearne's creative writing class at the University of the West Indies in the fall of 1990 not knowing what to expect. Up to that point, I wasn't even aware that creative writing could be taught, but couldn't figure out how to move beyond slavish imitations of Henry Fielding and Charles Dickens, with the occasional comic book bang! and pow! and some soap-opera melodrama thrown in. I had no idea what a creative writing class would be like, or even what kind of writing one would consider creative. At that point I could barely distinguish between creative prose and purple prose, and thought an outlandish sentence was some display of superior skill, or at least vocabulary.

All I knew of John Hearne was that he was a local columnist famous for his acerbic views, that he might have written a novel or two, and those novels I was probably confusing with the work of Roger Mais. Before I stepped into his class, the only other thing I knew about Hearne was that those novels were under-read. To paraphrase a professor, only John Hearne wrote about the white and brown Jamaican middle class, but nobody was reading him.

He was the kind of man you mistook as frail, until that booming voice came out. For my first story (I think it was called "Sin Eater") he pinpointed what would, even now, be my best and worst traits in prose: a knack for narrative economy, and a propensity for overheat. Or what another professor would call narrative theatre. It's a distinctly post-colonial condition where verbosity was (and is) looked upon as a kind of intellectual hallmark. And just about every writer coming out of British colonialism and post-colonialism struggles with it, the fight to resist inserting that fifteen-letter word where the six-letter word would do. An unabashed love for the darlings that American and Scandinavians novelists are so expert at killing.

But back to the day Hearne tore my piece apart. It was two weeks after I submitted a story where he almost ran out of words to praise, which is saying something coming from John Hearne. He talked about my way with metaphor and symbolism, my throwing crucial elements of the story to the characters, and my ability to push to the very edge the boundaries of melodrama and taste. No surprise, then, that for the following story, I doubled down on everything he liked, going for bigger, harder, faster and more. It was an atrocious story, where instead of pushing the door open a little more, I ripped it off the hinges with mixed and double-mixed metaphors, objects overworking as symbols, lines of prose that had fallen in love with themselves in between bouts of pornographic, sadomasochistic sex. They fell from such a height and continued having sex? I'm surprised one of them isn't dead, he said, or something close to that. The lesson was hard and clear: It what you don't say that leaves the biggest stain, not what you do.

It took me quite while to go from listening to Hearne to reading him, because whenever I took that writing hat off to go back to reading, I always remembered what my lit professor said about this being a new Caribbean reality, and that nobody was reading about the upper middle class. There are of course reasons for this, and most of them are legitimate. Even in this new millennium, writers such as Haitian Edwidge Danticat, and Jamaicans Nicole Dennis-Benn and Kei Miller are responding to erasure, a huge shortage in our stories being told because nobody thought to include us. But writers such as John Hearne in prose, and Louis Simpson in poetry, were responding to an erasure of a different kind, the post-independence, slightly revisionist idea that the upper middle class, the Caribbean white and near-white voice was illegitimate in the late twentieth century. This was the voice tied to colony, privilege, oppression and all those things British that we were trying to get away from.

This is of course untrue. There are huge differences between a colonial apologist (and horrible writer) like Herbert G. De Lisser, who wrote *The White Witch of Rose Hall* and other mulatto-sex-machine-gone-berserk romances, and pre/post-colonial complicators like John Hearne. In that sense Hearne is closer to Louis Simpson and Jean Rhys, who found no comfort in skin either. Or even Roger Mais, who translated this into a near rebellion from his own class. But where things always seem clear for Mais, it was always murky and difficult for Hearne.

Voices under the Window reflects this difficulty. It is a novel ill at ease with itself. Uneasy with politics and the questioning of politics, uneasy with the shifting dynamics of light skin, not exactly white but certainly not black either, uneasy with the shifting into whiteness that most of his peers found quite easy. It is a novel that runs from a political conscience, even as it grapples with the in-your-face reality of it. That might be one of the reasons why some of his peers (including Mais) questioned the work even as others such as T.S. Elliot embraced it. But that unease, the Hearne unease, is crucial to his work.

The main character, Lattimer, saves a boy from being trampled by a rioting crowd, but even this action is private; saving one person instead of a movement. The action costs him dearly and thrusts him into that no man's land where "the black people are bellowing at me to get off their necks, and the whites too". But while Lattimer insists that he is white, as so many Jamaicans did and still do, the novel recognizes that the claim isn't much more than a peculiarly British colonial condition, one that many would learn, to their shock, did not apply to the mother country when they got there. At the end of the novel is failure. Lattimer has a vision he cannot articulate, which was the novel's way of saying this important work would be done by others who cannot afford his deeply conflicted passivity.

Which of course made the novel a conflicting experience to read. It pushed nuance to the centre of the discussion at a time when nuance was possibly the last thing anyone wanted to read. It was too easy to write it off as the author's own passivity, especially with the stakes raised in the novels of George Lamming, and V.S. Naipaul in the Caribbean, Chinua Achebe and Amos Tutuola on the continent, not to mention other voices arising in the British colonial diaspora, such as Samuel Selvon. But more than that, those writers were writing novels of emergence whereas Hearne was writing from a class that had little to aspire to and much to maintain. This, even then, put him at an unusual position in West Indian letters. That of a moralist (not to be confused with moralizer), with a concern for social values beyond political allegiances or movements. Of someone pushing the concern for the individual over the group and, as he wrote, a political novel with "politics below the surface".

It is tempting to classify Hearne's Cayuna novels, his novels set in a fictional country, with Marquez's Macondo, Faulkner's Yoknapatawpha County or, more recently, Colin Channer's San Carlos – writers who in order to get to a closer reality invent a fictional landscape. In these cases, distancing one from some of the socio-political realities was the point. It was necessary in order to, as Hearne says, tell a new side of truth about the real world. Because to tell these truths, one does need elaborate fictions, places that are really just wide and stretchable canvases that can allow for all the fictions, including the fantastical or the alternative history, to tell secret histories. Grand lies that tell bigger truths.

Which is not to say these fictions were always successful. The problem with spinning a new reality is that you can come to a conclusion less real. Complex problems are sometimes given too-simple solutions and characters move from being people to archetypes, some representing an ideal of the author that verges on romanticism. One could also take issue with his looking at the black and the white experience of slavery as two sides of the same shared coin, or the view that it was shared at all; a view not held by many now (and was certainly challenged then), but perhaps a necessary belief for a community of privilege.

But there is something to be said about fiction that dares to cover an intimate space as much as, if not more than, a social one. And to dismiss Hearne as a middle-class novelist is to ignore, among other things, the rise of a new middle class. Not as white or near-white as in his day, but many of the concerns remain the same, and in the present day there is a huge void in our collective Caribbean literature that speaks to these private realities, sometimes outside of public events, sometimes shaped by them. That while we are constantly replenished by poetry of poverty, many times without nuance, what we might be lacking is work reflective of the space that many writers actually live in. Maybe we have earned the right to the novel that explores uptown Kingston in no other context than uptown Kingston. It's already happening, here in the United States and elsewhere in the diaspora, where the white (or near-white character) is neither a tool to drum up international sales, a caricature to be held in mild contempt over their moral laziness, or just a symbol of a still-dying era of colonial colour, but characters in their own three dimensionality, living in their own space, with too much complexity and conflict to be reduced to just an issue.

But as we make room for these kinds of novels, short stories, poems, plays and biographies, it is crucial to remember that in this and many regards, John Hearne got there first.

Preface

This volume brings together John Hearne's short stories in a single collection for the first time. Although most of the stories were previously published, they appeared in smaller journals and some anthologies between 1953 and 1994 and they are not easily available. In organizing this collection, I have for the most part followed a chronological order of when the stories were published, deviating from that only where I have evidence of the story being written earlier.

John Hearne left Jamaica in 1943 at the age of seventeen to enlist in the Royal Air Force. Following the Second World War, he remained in the United Kingdom to attend university, first the University of Edinburgh and then the University of London's Institute of Education. He returned briefly to Jamaica from 1950 to 1952 before leaving for England again, where he felt he would find a more culturally and creatively fulfilling life. (He was as much drawn by the significant people in his life who were in London: Leeta Hopkinson, the love of his life, whom he would later marry, and his dear friend Roger Mais.)[1]

Hearne was determined to be recognized internationally as a writer and the first signs of that recognition came soon after his return to London when his fable "The Mongoose Who Came to the City" appeared in the *New Statesman and Nation* (45, no. 1160 [30 May 1953]: 640).[2] This was his first published piece and a significant accomplishment for an unknown writer. (Two months later, his poem "Black Boy in a New World" appeared in the *New Statesman* [46, no. 1165 (4 July 1953): 12].) "The Bridge" would appear the following year in a small literary journal, *Departure* (2, no. 6 [Winter 1954]: 7–12), but by early 1954 Hearne was growing frustrated by publishers' lack of interest in the novel that would become *Voices under the Window*.

He moved between writing poetry and prose, reading widely all the while. In one creative phase in February 1954, he wrote three short stories: "A Village Tragedy", "Ramon" and "The Haitian Admiral". Of these, only "A Village Tragedy" was published (*Atlantic*, November 1958, 63–68).[3] I have never found manuscripts for "Ramon" or "The Haitian Admiral".

By September 1954 Hearne's first novel, *Voices under the Window*, had been accepted by Faber and Faber and it was published in September 1955. This was the recognition he had craved, but by the end of 1955 Hearne felt restless and ready for adventure. He had applied unsuccessfully for teaching positions at schools in Africa and India before recognizing that it was the Caribbean that he felt most drawn towards, and in March 1956 he was on a banana boat bound for Jamaica.

The two years that followed in Jamaica were remarkably fertile and fulfilling for Hearne. He returned to find a far more vibrant arts scene than he had left in 1952. His short story "Morning, Noon and Night" appeared in *Focus*, edited by Edna Manley (Kingston: Extra Mural Department, University College of the West Indies, 1956), and was likely written soon after his return to Jamaica in 1956.

Between 1956 and 1958, Hearne taught high school, lectured occasionally on literature, and wrote regularly for *Pagoda*, the *Daily Gleaner* and *Spotlight*. One assignment for *Spotlight* gave him the opportunity, for the first time, to travel widely in the Caribbean and explore the rest of the region. (See the appendix, "From a Journal", for extracts from Hearne's notes on his travels in the 1950s.) Guyana (at the time still British Guiana) in particular captivated him, and what is perhaps his strongest short story, "At the Stelling" (*Atlantic*, November 1960, 90–96), was written out of this period,[4] as was "The Lost Country" (*Atlantic*, September 1961, 64–69).

By mid-1958, however, Hearne was restless again and ready to return to England to take up a job teaching at Midhurst Grammar School. His novels *Stranger at the Gate* (1956) and *Faces of Love* (1957) had appeared in quick succession, to enthusiastic reviews, and his fourth novel, *The Autumn Equinox,* would be published in 1959. He felt that in England, he could live off his writing alone. By 1960 this was in fact the case: he was writing teleplays and radio plays for ITV and the BBC and working on his fifth novel, *Land of the Living* (1961).

Despite his success in England he was beginning to find the place dull. Once again, Hearne felt his place was in the Caribbean, confirming "the intuition that has been nagging me for the last year: that there is no other place for me now, either as a citizen or an artist".[5]

Although Hearne was never active in party politics, he had always been deeply engaged with the dynamics of political activity and loyalty, which we see "The Wind in This Corner" (*Atlantic*, May 1960, 53–59).[6] The pull of Jamaica was particularly strong on the eve of independence and when Norman Manley, leader of the People's National Party and a close friend, asked Hearne to join the Jamaica Information Service he returned to Jamaica for the last time. His writing from then on was largely non-fiction.[7] It would take him close to twenty years to finish his last novel, *The Sure Salvation* (1981).

Hearne had left the Jamaica Information Service when the People's National Party lost the 1962 elections, and from that point on Hearne taught at the University of the West Indies in the Department of Extra-Mural Studies and then from 1967 on as head of the newly established Creative Arts Centre (now the Philip Sherlock Centre for the Creative Arts). He also had steady work as a journalist, appearing as a commentator on radio and television, writing a regular column for the *Daily Gleaner*, and occasionally contributing articles to international publications.

Apart from two years, 1972 to 1974, spent working with the People's National Party at the Agency for Public Information and the Office of the Prime Minister, Hearne would spend the rest of his career at the University of the West Indies, teaching creative writing and journalism until his retirement in 1992.

In the early 1990s, there was a flicker of overseas interest in Hearne's work. "At the Stelling" was staged by an alternative theatre company in Los Angeles in early 1993 and later that year he was invited to submit a short story to the anthology *Fiery Spirits: Canadian Writers of African Descent,*[8] edited by Ayanna Black (Toronto: HarperPerennial, 1994). That story was "Living Out the Winter", written much earlier – likely in the late 1950s or early 1960s – and never published.

The only unpublished story in this collection is "Reckonings". I found this typescript among his papers and the only element that dates it is that Guyana is referred to as such, rather than British Guiana, which would place it after Guyanese independence in 1966. There was a 1970 rejection letter from the *Atlantic*,[9] and an undated rejection letter from the *Spectator*, to whom Hearne had submitted the story under the odd pseudonym "Angela Saumarez".

Finally, the non-fiction piece "From a Journal" (*Tamarack Review* 14 [Winter 1960]: 133–42) is included here as an appendix for the context it gives to the period in which these stories were written. It reflects Hearne's burst of creative energy in his twenties and early thirties, his sense of wonder and his love of the arts. Also evident is his awareness of inhabiting a pivotal moment in Caribbean history and of the dynamics of race, class and politics that would be at the foundation of nation-building in the region. These dynamics are present in his fiction writing as well, and his short stories and novels capture a moment in twentieth-century Caribbean history that needs to be more fully understood as we navigate our postcolonial reality.

John Hearne is remembered today more as a journalist and for the influence he had on generations of writers, academics and students – as friend, colleague and teacher – than for his creative writing. But these connections were not the extent of his reach: his fiction must be included in any serious consideration of the region's literature. In his writing, he was "alone on his own road // his prose rustling from a tall cedar",[10] and that road without question cut through the heart of the Caribbean.

S.H.

NOTES

1. For a fuller biography of Hearne's early life, see Shivaun Hearne, *John Hearne's Life and Fiction: A Critical Biographical Study* (Kingston: Caribbean Quarterly, 2013).

2. This story caught the attention of anthropologist Sidney Mintz, who did extensive work in the Caribbean: "Both politically and, to a lesser extent, literarily, the Caribbean was already quite distinctive when I began working there, fifty years ago. I cannot now remember just what year it was, but I'd read a wonderful little story in the *New Statesman and Nation* called 'The Mongoose Who Came to the City', by a West Indian writer. I filed it away and forgot the name of its author. And a couple of years ago I saw John Hearne in Washington, DC, and told him – I cannot now remember what jogged my memory – I said to him, 'By the way, I read an extremely interesting story by a British West Indian writer years ago, and maybe you know about it,' and I named the story. He gave me an extremely funny look, and he said 'That's the first thing I ever published!'" Sidney W. Mintz, "Routes to the Caribbean: An Interview with Sidney W. Mintz", by Ashraf Ghani, *Plantation Society in the Americas* 5, no. 1 (1998): 120–21.

3. "A Village Tragedy" was reprinted in *Suspense* 3, no. 12 (December 1960): 28–40; *Stories from the Caribbean*, edited by Andrew Salkey, 15–26 (London: Elek Books, 1965) (later published as *Island Voices: Stories from the West Indies* [New York: Liveright, 1970]) and in *From the Green Antilles,* edited by Barbara Howes, 27–39 (London: Souvenir Press, 1967).

4. "At the Stelling" was reprinted in *West Indian Stories*, edited by Andrew Salkey, 51–68 (London: Faber and Faber, 1960) and *Best West Indian Stories*, edited by Kenneth Ramchand, 67–80 (Walton-on-Thames: Nelson Caribbean, 1982).

5. John Hearne, "An Émigré's Journal", 10 October 1961, typescript, 225.

6. "The Wind in This Corner" was reprinted in *West Indian Stories*, edited by Andrew Salkey, 69–87 (London: Faber and Faber, 1960); *Caribbean Literature,* edited by G.R. Coulthard, 38–54 (London: University of London, 1966); and *From the Green Antilles,* edited by Barbara Howes, 40–56 (London: Souvenir Press, 1967).

7. Hearne and friend Morris Cargill co-authored the pseudonymous "John Morris" novels in the hope that these would be commercially successful spy thrillers.

8. Hearne was Canadian by accident of birth. He lived in Montreal for the first two years of his life and was only in Canada thereafter for flight training for

the Royal Air Force and much later, in 1985–86, when he taught for two
semesters at Dalhousie University and the University of New Brunswick.

9. The letter from the *Atlantic* called the story "elegant and perceptive but not
    quite on our target". Phoebe-Lou Adams, letter to John Hearne, 4 June 1970.

10. Derek Walcott, "41: In Memoriam, John Hearne", in *White Egrets* (London:
    Faber and Faber, 2010). My thanks to Edward Baugh for drawing my attention
    to Walcott's exquisite tribute to Hearne.

Introduction

KIM ROBINSON-WALCOTT

When John Hearne's first novel, *Voices under the Window*, appeared in 1955,[1] he had already had two short stories published: "The Mongoose Who Came to the City" and "The Bridge" in 1953 and 1954 respectively.[2] Thereafter, he seems to have focused primarily on his larger projects: over the next six years, Hearne would publish nearly as many novels (four – the Cayuna series)[3] as stories (six).[4] Then came the dry period: for twenty years neither novel nor story appeared, until the 1981 publication of *The Sure Salvation*, his last novel.[5] In 1994, the year of his death, his final published story appeared: "Living Out the Winter".[6]

This collection consists primarily of the stories by Hearne published in the eight-year period 1953–61. The collection, compiled by Hearne's daughter Shivaun, ends with one unpublished story, "Reckonings", as well as a short piece, "From a Journal", included as an appendix.

For most of that eight-year period, Hearne was based in the United Kingdom.[7] Yet most of his stories published then, and indeed all his novels as well, are based in the Caribbean. Four out of the five novels published in that period are located in the fictional island of Cayuna, loosely based on Jamaica; his first novel, *Voices*, was located in Jamaica. Three out of the ten stories are located in Cayuna, two in Jamaica, two in a fictionalized version of what was then British Guiana, and one, the last published, in Trinidad. "From a Journal" presents fragments of thought as the author moves between Europe and the Caribbean, and the remaining story, "The

Bridge", is set in post-war Europe. Although at one point (in 1958) he claimed that returning to the United Kingdom had "cured [him] of the Caribbean" and that most of him was "lodged immovably in the European",[8] his writing – and indeed his eventual physical relocation to Jamaica in 1961 – indicated otherwise. Hearne said more than once that the Caribbean, or more specifically Jamaica, was "the page on which I must write . . . The one place I refer back to as by necessity".[9] And in reference to his time in the United Kingdom, he stated retrospectively in 1993 that "distancing was easier than if I lived [in Jamaica] . . . I could detach myself and look at it".[10] Hearne's eventual domicile in Jamaica would be remarked on later by one critic who referred to him as "one of the few novelists of his generation who stayed in the West Indies".[11] That final move back home in 1961, however, would ironically result, as indicated above, in an almost total cessation of his literary output.

When Hearne returned to Jamaica in late 1961, having established himself as a leading West Indian novelist heralded by critics as "the most accomplished of the new school of Caribbean writers",[12] it was at the invitation of then premier Norman Manley, leader of the ruling People's National Party (PNP), who asked him to take over the foreign-press portfolio of the Jamaica Information Service.[13] However, in April 1962 there was a change of government as a result of the PNP's loss in the general elections. Hearne, who openly stated his loyalty to the PNP and to Manley, resigned from the Jamaica Information Service, and in September 1962 joined the staff of the University of the West Indies at Mona. Importantly, he also started writing a weekly column for the *Gleaner*. This was the start of his career as a newspaper columnist; and as the decade, as well as the following one, progressed, his creative energies were increasingly channelled into this activity. Hearne also began to suffer bouts of depression, and the beginnings of alcoholism. His depression may have been at least partly due to his plunge in status from acclaimed writer to pariah in the late 1960s when his writing was attacked by several West Indian critics, notably George Lamming and Sylvia Wynter, as being too middle-class in orientation, not progressive enough or sufficiently representative of the Jamaican or West Indian peasantry.[14] Such criticism came at a time when Hearne and his friend, the journalist Morris Cargill, had embarked on a project of writing a popular fiction series under the pseudonym John Morris. They published three novels: the first, *Fever Grass* (1969), did well commercially and there was foreign interest in film rights, but the second and third, *The Candywine Development* (1970) and *The Checkerboard Caper* (1975), were less successful.[15] Hearne increasingly questioned his own relevance as a writer, and the predictable result was a dearth of creative writing. In 1970 he submitted the short story "Reckonings" to the *Atlantic*, and when it was rejected, he submitted it to another journal using a female pseudonym. That journal also rejected it.[16] Conceivably shattered by this double rejection and determined to restore his status as acclaimed writer, Hearne thereafter became obsessed with writing "the great novel".[17] It took another eleven years before that novel, *The Sure Salvation*, was published; and although it received critical recognition, it never received the level of acclaim that Hearne had sought. Hearne's short stories, then, though not major in terms of quantity, nevertheless play a key role in the story of his creative output.

HEARNE'S MORAL IDEALIST STORYTELLING

The two best known, and among the most outstanding, stories in this collection are "The Wind in This Corner" and "At the Stelling". Both were first published in 1960, and both were included in well-known anthologies.[18] "The Wind in This Corner", set in Cayuna, zooms in on a group of politicians who travel to the country home of their party leader to give him the unpleasant news that they wish him to step down from his position as leader. Hearne's depiction of the "Old Man", noble, dignified, gracious in his defeat and heartbreak, recalls values and ideals demonstrated time and again in his novels – recalling, for example, the Cayuna landowner Carl Brandt first introduced to us in *Stranger at the Gate*, or even the Haitian exile Pierre-Auguste in *Autumn Equinox*. Those heroic qualities were hinted at in the portrayal of the army officer Ian MacAlla, the protagonist in Hearne's early work "The Bridge", a story of postwar recognition of loss.

"At the Stelling" was, according to Derek Walcott, Hearne's "most memorable" story, displaying "the same seismographic gift of recording eruptions of character, gentle shiftings of social attitudes, and changes of landscape" as his novels.[19] "At the Stelling" is set in the interior of a country resembling British Guiana, and addresses dichotomies of geography, race and class. Dunnie, the first-person narrator, relates the conflict between an arrogant mulatto boss, Mister Cockburn, and his Amerindian worker, John, as they travel into the interior while doing a survey. Cockburn, recruited from the town, is new in the position, unused to the landscape, and insecure, "frighten": he cannot handle any perceived insubordination; nor does he have the cultural understanding to enable him to be sensitive to the perspective of his employee. John, suffering from the loss of his former boss, Mr Hamilton, who understood and respected him, is a man of the interior, an expert hunter, and cannot understand why Cockburn refuses to allow him to carry a rifle. For John, hunting, and therefore possession of the rifle, is representative of his manhood; for Cockburn, the rifle is a symbol of his own authority, and John's defiance is an assault on his own manhood. As the days and weeks pass, the tension between the two men mounts, and culminates in tragedy when Cockburn's humiliation of John causes an excessively violent reaction. In spare prose, a style compared by several critics to that of Hemingway (as indeed has been his depiction of his male heroes),[20] Hearne leads us on a trek into the interior, but more so, into a dark psychological place.

The interior, and the dichotomies explored in "At the Stelling", feature again in the story "The Lost Country". When the Carib-Scottish protagonist, the surveyor Harry Hamilton (presumably the same Mr Hamilton who featured peripherally as Cockburn's predecessor in "At the Stelling"), is forced to stop work in the interior for health reasons, he is distressed that he "will have to spend the rest of [his] days on this stinking coast". "That's a death sentence," he tells the doctor. Harry subsequently finds ways of making short trips into the interior as often as possible, and on one trip finds a black worker, Bargie, who is gravely ill and must be carried back to the coast for medical attention. The doctor tells Harry that in the unlikely event Bargie recovers, he must not be allowed to return to the interior because "he could never survive another month in the bush". But Harry knows that those from the coast will never understand that "we are lost without something like the interior":

The ancestral heritage greater and more precious than any one race or one history or one hope. Too intense and too real to be encountered directly. Only to be seen from the corner of the eye in the way that the Indians are born knowing, that Bargie learned, that I was learning. How to tell it, my God? And how to tell that it will be perceptible in our later isolation as the elusive, half-remembered fragment of some enormous, receding and unpossessable dream?

Harry's mixed Carib-Scottish heritage is significant here because it enables Harry to approach (though not necessarily to attain) an understanding of the ancestral heritage represented in the interior, while at the same time it enables him to attempt (though not necessarily successfully) to articulate its meaning to the Europeans on the coast. This is additionally significant if we return to "At the Stelling" where Mr Hamilton features as the former, more benevolent and sensitive leader. Wilson Harris had expressed disappointment with the "moral directive" of that story because of its "relationship between master and servant": Harris, assuming that Hamilton is full European, accuses Hearne of constructing a scenario where the Carib John shoots the mulatto Cockburn and order is restored by the white Hamilton and white superintendent of police.[21] However, the perspective provided to us from an assumption that the two Hamiltons are one and the same person complicates Harris's view.

One critic of Hearne's novels has rightly observed that his emphasis "is on the moral dilemmas of his characters" who "are deeply aware of the vulnerability of their own cultural inheritance and the disintegration of traditional values"; that observation also applies to his stories. The same critic notes that Hearne has been called a "moral idealist", and suggests that "the particular plight of [the characters in his novels] is naturally determined by the issues at the centre of Jamaican life: race, colour, educational aspiration and the economic structure of a society in transition".[22] Indeed, although most of the stories are not Jamaica- or Cayuna-based, their moral idealism — certainly, that of the best pieces — may in fact originate from or be sensitized by that base.

HEARNE THE PAN-CARIBBEANIST

Hearne's brief stint in British Guiana and countries of the eastern Caribbean in 1957, reporting on Federation for Jamaica's *Spotlight* magazine,[23] clearly had a profound impact on him, as demonstrated by "At the Stelling" and "The Lost Country". Walcott would note in a 1961 *Trinidad Guardian* column: "Formerly an anti-federationist, he now accepts the Federation as inevitable and necessary. He plans to return to live in Jamaica, perhaps, permanently, because he feels that the West Indies is among the most exciting places in the world for a writer to be."[24]

Hearne's embracing of Federation would undoubtedly have been influenced by his admiration of Jamaica's premier Norman Manley, a staunch federationist. His outlook would develop further from federationist to pan-Caribbeanist, as shown especially in the Cayuna novels *Stranger at the Gate* and *Autumn Equinox*, where the anglophone Cayuna's social and political links with the Hispanic Caribbean and Haiti are promoted as both desirable and real. Many years later, Hearne would return to Guyana, followed by Trinidad, as the setting of his last published story, "Living Out the Winter". Kate Houlden refers to Hearne's "expansive Caribbean vision"[25] and, more so, to "his attraction to a 'New World' model of belonging based on ideas of regional unity, creolization, and creativity".[26] "Living Out the Winter", in its movement from one Caribbean territory to the next, is a prime example of Hearne's conception of such regional unity, creolization and creativity. The protagonist, a West Indian (likely Jamaican) writer, decides he has stayed long enough in Guyana and so moves on to Trinidad, where he decides to live out the winter: "I don't think I want to go to Jamaica just now, and going back to England wouldn't be a very good idea at the moment. I'll stay here." He leaves Guyana because "the East Indians and the Africans between them were tearing the place to pieces", but not because he was not made welcome there: "Their manners, their sense of honourable obligation to a stranger, their sweet and courteous exchanges did not belong, it seemed to me, to the age around us but to some fine, archaic inspiration of chivalry. Now, they still took time out from killing each other by inches to press with gentle insistence gifts of food, attention, self on me."

In Trinidad, his welcome is just as warm, as he is embraced by a married couple, the Ramesars, whom he meets for the first time when he rents a room in their home.

> They both made the house such a good place to live and work in, treating me not like a friend . . . but as a member of the family. . . . You won't really understand us in the West Indies until you understand our habit of adopting into some sort of kin relationship whoever sleeps under your roof for more than a couple of nights . . . [I]t stems, simply, from the fact that to be a West Indian is a damned lonely business and that we are always looking for ways to alleviate our loneliness.

In the Ramesars' home, waiting out the winter as he waits for his wife in England to forgive him for the hurt he has caused her, the writer then becomes witness to – and partial instigator of – the slow dissolution of the couple's marriage.

A SOCIETY IN TRANSITION

Hearne's astute observations of racial dynamics in Trinidad and in the couple's relationship add a dynamic to "Living Out the Winter" which was also evident in the earlier stories. There is some evidence of excitement with the possibility of hybridity – whether black–East Indian, as in the case of Elaine Ramesar, one of those *douglahs* "with skins the texture and colour of the icing on a chocolate cake, vivid, troubling faces, and coarse, straight hair like the manes of black horses" (recalling the "new beauty and vigour" of a mixed-race woman described in *Land of the Living*), or white-Amerindian, as in the case of Harry Hamilton in "The Lost Country". The excitement may betray some ambivalence – in the description of Elaine Ramesar we note the word "troubling" and her comparison to an animal. However, for the most part, Hearne's stories seem to embrace a new creolized future reality while accurately recording the racial tensions, ambivalences and divisions existing in a Caribbean society in transition, be it in British Guiana, Trinidad, Cayuna or Jamaica.

Sometimes the stories suggest a tolerance of difference underlying the surface bigotry: in "The Lost Country", for example, the black Bargie and, especially, the East Indian Stephen make derogatory references to each other's race, but the story reveals an underlying "curious and touching" deep affection and caring for each other. The politicians in "The Wind in This Corner" make joking references to the usefulness of the race card:

> "He's beginning to frighten the government now, so Gomez decided to use [the white opponent's] colour against him."
> "Lack of colour, you mean," the Old Man said with delight. "Good. That's what I like to hear. Black Man's Party. White Man's Party. Jew Man's Party. Chinaman's Party. They'll soon run out of labels. Each time they clap another one on us, it means we're hurting them somewhere."

Class divisions may be more invidious. And there can be no denying that Hearne's stories, like his novels, mostly present a middle- or upper-class perspective in which the poor black person is othered – thus opening him up to a barrage of criticism from Caribbean/West Indian critics in the late 1960s – principally, Lamming and Wynter – who wished his work to speak more directly to, and on behalf of, the condition of the poor black majority. With the possible exception of the curious early fable "The Mongoose Who Came to the City" (assuming that the mongoose represents a poor black Jamaican), the only story in this collection that features a poor black protagonist – "Morning, Noon and Night" – still includes the figure of the (mulatto) middle-class benefactor, Gerald Hayes, as the only positive influence in the struggling poor black Reuben's life. Class, as it always does in the Caribbean context, conflates with colour: when Reuben is persuaded to turn to crime, his victims are "very fair brown" and one of them calls him a "goddam black bitch". Reuben's hopeless future makes this the most depressing story in this collection. "A Village Tragedy" also features a poor black principal character, this time the "natural" (mentally disabled) Joseph; but despite Hearne's obvious sympathy to the character, Joseph is somewhat caricatured as village idiot, and it is the higher-class Reverend Mackinnon and even higher-class (with his own manservant) Doctor Rushdie who are the voices of reason in the village.

Nevertheless, most of Hearne's stories brim with social awareness and critique the inadequate class/race structure that is the inheritance of colonialism. The one exception to this is the only story that was never published. "Reckonings" relates the death of a successful and well-to-do writer, discovered by his manservant; his legitimate daughter and illegitimate son attempt to come to terms with his life and his death. "He was born lucky," his daughter says. "Things always seemed to go right for him. Friends, houses, travel, money, children, recognition. He never wanted for anything in his life. Even death didn't break the run." However, they too have reckonings of their own. These reckonings, however, restricted to the well-off and comfortable sister-brother pair, perhaps may not stir the reader as much as do the conflicts and challenges portrayed in the other stories.

What is of particular interest here, nevertheless, is the depiction of Renfrew, the deceased writer. Successful as he was, he was a womanizer and had a troubled relationship with his daughter, and practically no relationship with his son. Neither child will continue the family name of Renfrew. The tarnished depiction recalls that of the writer in "Living Out the Winter" – not as successful careerwise, perhaps, but also flawed in his relationships with his women and with his friends. It is tempting to read these depictions as Hearne's partial views of himself; and certainly the aspect of troubled relationships with women and family relates to Hearne's own life.

On the other hand, the writer in "Living Out the Winter" is congratulated by Victor Ramesar: "You been writing some great books, man. Just what we need in the West Indies. Our own people writing from the inside about us." And although the writer demurs, saying, "I'm not a famous writer. I'm just one of a lot of writers trying to get famous", that moment of recognition is, for that writer, clearly one of the few pleasurable moments in a long, depressing winter.

LIVING OUT THE WINTER

In those eleven years between the rejection of "Reckonings" and the disappointingly moderate acclaim of *Sure Salvation*, Hearne's life became increasingly challenging. In 1972, Norman Manley's son Michael became prime minister, and in 1974 Michael asked Hearne to chair the new government agency, the Agency for Public Information. Hearne plunged into this job, ill-advisedly resigning from the University of the West Indies to take it up, and when it did not work out after eight months, moved to a new position as special assistant to the prime minister. However, by 1976 Hearne (like many middle-class Jamaicans) began to feel disillusioned with Manley and with politics, and returned to the university. According to Shivaun Hearne, he "became more involved in investigative journalism and . . . more critical of Manley and the government in his column".[27] In September 1977 he was attacked by PNP supporters, and this led to the final rift between Hearne and the PNP. It was only after that, Shivaun Hearne notes, that Hearne was able to turn his energies once more to his creative writing, to complete the manuscript of *The Sure Salvation*. When Hearne saw that the critical reception to the novel was lukewarm, he plunged further into depression and alcoholism. In the next decade he produced no new creative work, publishing only "Living Out the Winter", which had been written many years earlier. For Hearne, that period was his own personal winter.

When Hearne died in 1994 he was a defeated man, disillusioned by politics and the perceived treachery of Michael Manley, hurt by his rejection from the West Indian literary canon, beset by personal demons and disappointments. It was a fate he did not deserve. The accolades that he had earlier received, for his stories as well as his novels, were justified. The stylistic comparisons to Hemingway made by those early critics are apt: his style is indeed "clean, pared"; his male protagonists are also reminiscent of Hemingway in their nobility, bravery and moral idealism; his social commentary is nuanced yet incisive in its recording of "gentle shiftings of social attitudes"; his descriptions of landscape are magnificent. If his worldview sometimes seems colonial and dated in his novels, that is not the case in the majority of his short stories. Indeed, politically, his pan-Caribbean views were ahead of his time; and his embracing of a pan-Caribbean vision resulted in three of his strongest stories – the ones set in British Guiana and Trinidad.

These stories, then, presented together for the first time in one published collection, provide a new perspective on John Hearne the writer as well as helping to resuscitate old forgotten perspectives. There have been recent glimmerings of interest on the part of a few scholars in re-examining Hearne's literary oeuvre. Hopefully this collection will further encourage a revisiting of his position, to return him to a secure place within the Caribbean literary canon.

NOTES

1. John Hearne, *Voices under the Window* (1955; London: Faber and Faber, 1973).

2. John Hearne, "The Mongoose Who Came to the City", *New Statesman and Nation* 45, no. 1160 (30 May 1953): 640; "The Bridge", *Departure* 2, no. 6 (Winter 1954): 7–12.

3. John Hearne's four Cayuna novels were *Stranger at the Gate* (London: Faber and Faber, 1956); *The Faces of Love* (London: Faber and Faber, 1957); *Autumn Equinox* (London: Faber and Faber, 1959); *Land of the Living* (London: Faber and Faber, 1961).

4. John Hearne, "Morning, Noon and Night", in *Focus*, ed. Edna Manley (Kingston, Jamaica: Extra Mural Department, University College of the West Indies, 1956), 1–12; "Village Tragedy", *Atlantic*, November 1958, 63–68; "The Wind in This Corner", *Atlantic*, May 1960, 53–59; "At the Stelling", *Atlantic*, November 1960, 90–96; "From a Journal", *Tamarack Review* 14 (Winter 1960): 133–42; "The Lost Country", *Atlantic*, September 1961, 64–69.

5. The exception in this dry period was a series of three works of popular fiction co-authored with Morris Cargill and published between 1969 and 1975 under the pseudonym "John Morris". These works, intended as a commercial venture, fall outside the body of Hearne's literary oeuvre. *The Sure Salvation* was published in London by Faber and Faber in 1981 and in New York by St Martin's in 1982.

6. John Hearne, "Living Out the Winter", in *Fiery Spirits: Canadian Writers of African Descent*, ed. Ayanna Black (Toronto: HarperPerennial, 1994), 72–99.

7. Hearne left Jamaica in 1943 to fight in World War II. When the war ended he entered Edinburgh University where he completed two degrees by 1949, followed by a diploma of education at the University of London which he finished in 1950, after which he returned to Jamaica. Two years later he returned to London, where he lived for the next four years. In 1956 he again moved back to Jamaica; on this occasion he stayed two years before returning to London. His final exit from London was in 1961; thereafter Jamaica became his permanent home. See Shivaun Hearne, *John Hearne's Life and Fiction* (Kingston: Caribbean Quarterly, University of the West Indies, 2013), chapters 3–4.

8. Shivaun Hearne, *John Hearne's Life and Fiction*, 45.

9. Ibid., 30.

10. Ibid., 45.

11. Hena Maes-Jelinek, "The Novel from 1950 to 1970", in *A History of*

Literature in the Caribbean, vol. 2: *English- and Dutch-Speaking Regions*, ed. A. James Arnold (Amsterdam/Philadelphia: John Benjamins, 2001), 134.

12. John Davenport, review of *The Faces of Love*, *London Sunday Observer*, 28 April 1957, 13. See also B. Evan Owen, review of *Stranger at the Gate*, *Oxford Mail*, 10 May 1956; Edward (Kamau) Brathwaite, review of *Autumn Equinox*, *Bim* 8, no. 31 (July–December 1960): 216; G.R. Coulthard, *Caribbean Literature: An Anthology* (London: University of London Press, 1966), 38; among others.

13. Shivaun Hearne, *John Hearne's Life and Fiction*, 58.

14. See George Lamming, *The Pleasures of Exile* (1960; repr., Ann Arbor: University of Michigan Press, 1992), 45–46; Sylvia Wynter, "We Must Learn to Sit Down Together and Talk about a Little Culture: Reflections on West Indian Writing and Criticism", part 2, *Jamaica Journal* 3, no. 1 (March 1969): 37; see also, Kim Robinson-Walcott, "John Hearne: Beyond the Plantation", in *Beyond Windrush: Rethinking Postwar Anglophone Caribbean Literature*, ed. J. Dillon Brown and Leah Reade Rosenberg (Jackson: University Press of Mississippi, 2015), 158–75.

15. John Morris, *Fever Grass* (New York: Putnams, 1969; Kingston: Collins and Sangster 1969); *The Candywine Development* (London: Collins, 1970; New York: Citadel, 1970); *The Checkerboard Caper* (New York: Citadel, 1975).

16. Shivaun Hearne, *John Hearne's Life and Fiction*, 57.

17. Ibid., 68.

18. "At the Stelling" was reprinted in *Best West Indian Stories*, ed. Kenneth Ramchand (Walton-on-Thames: Nelson Caribbean, 1982), 67–80; "The Wind in This Corner" was reprinted in *West Indian Stories*, ed. Andrew Salkey (London: Faber and Faber, 1960), 69–87, then in *From the Green Antilles*, ed. Barbara Howes (London: Souvenir Press, 1967), 40–56, as well as in *Caribbean Literature*, ed. G.R. Coulthard (London: University of London, 1966), 38–54. Note that "A Village Tragedy" was also reprinted in two anthologies: *From the Green Antilles*, 27–39 and *Island Voices: Stories from the West Indies*, ed. Andrew Salkey (New York: Liveright, 1970 – originally published as *Stories from the Caribbean* [London: Elek Books, 1965]), 15–26.

19. Derek Walcott, "Novelist Hearne Possesses Neat, Disciplined Style", *Sunday Guardian*, 3 September 1961, repr. in *Derek Walcott, The Journeyman Years: Occasional Prose 1957–1974*, vol. 1: *Culture, Society, Literature and Art*, ed. Gordon Collier (Amsterdam/New York: Rodopi, 2013), 263.

20. For example: "This is reinforced by a neat, disciplined style whose origins are in Hemingway, but which Hearne is beginning to make his own" (Walcott,

"Novelist Hearne", 263); "Hearne's prose, clean and pared, recalls Hemingway's" (Victor J. Ramraj, "Short Fiction", in Arnold, *A History of Literature*, 209). Also: "The idealism of Hearne's major characters and their connections with nature have often been compared to Hemingway's" (Maes-Jelinek, "The Novel from 1950 to 1970", 135).

21. Wilson Harris, *Selected Essays of Wilson Harris: The Unfinished Genesis of the Imagination*, intro. and ed. A.J.M. Bundy (London: Routledge, 1999), 142.

22. Maes-Jelinek, "The Novel from 1950 to 1970", 135.

23. Shivaun Hearne, *John Hearne's Life and Fiction*, 43–44.

24. Walcott, "Novelist Hearne", 264.

25. Kate Houlden, "John Hearne's Plantation Fantasy", in Brown and Reade Rosenberg, *Beyond Windrush*, 152. Houlden suggests that such a regional vision was tempered by his plantation nostalgia.

26. Ibid., 151.

27. Shivaun Hearne, *John Hearne's Life and Fiction*, 71.

The Mongoose Who Came to the City

(A Fable)

There was a mongoose once, and he lived in the country in Jamaica with his Mammy and his Daddy. He was a pretty good son, too.

Breeze-blow, cloud-burst or drought, he kept his aged parents well supplied with fresh-killed chicken, and sometimes a fat duck or guinea-hen.

One day he came home with a plump tender Leghorn, and they all ate it to a polished skeleton. But, afterwards, Mongoose, instead of going to sleep, kept prowling and twisting in the cave, while his parents watched him with worried expressions.

"What's troublin' you, boy?" said his Daddy. "Is it love?"

"It ain't love," said his Mammy. "It's itchy feet. I seen it before. When you get it, there ain't but one thing to do. Watch!"

Before they could say, "Stop, boy," Mongoose was out of the cave, down the hillside; running fast to stop the itch in his feet.

Faster and faster he went, nose to the ground, through the cane fields and banana walks, and out on to the dusty rolling cattle lands. Then he took to the black asphalt road and kept running, not stopping at the water troughs, breathing in all the dust and dry dung till his throat was raw and burning.

At last he tripped over a gutter and rolled on to his back and sat up, his muscles twitching with tiredness. He was in a yard. Dust was blowing about in little, nasty clouds; there wasn't a blade of grass anywhere and all the houses were built of empty kerosene tins roofed with bits of packing case or even cardboard. A man was sitting on a box by the standpipe at the head of the gutter and smoking a queer-smelling, brown-paper cigarette.

"Good mawning, Mongoose," said the man, without showing any surprise. "You shore look tired out. You coming from far?"

"Good morning, sir," said Mongoose. "I am a little weary. I've been travelling hard since yesterday."

"What you need," said the man, "is a drag of the stuff." He offered Mongoose the cigarette. Mongoose took it politely, being country-bred.

"Where you goin', Mongoose?" asked the man as Mongoose puffed on the cigarette.

"Kingston," said Mongoose. "The great capital. The place where you see everybody in a motor car and everybody's got three pairs of shoes, one for walking in, one for dancing and one you just wear when you're sitting around. Kingston, man, where they eat fresh beef every day."

"Well, I've *heard* of that Kingston," said the man. "But *this* is the Kingston I know." And he waved his hand about the yard.

"Well, well," said Mongoose.

After a while Mongoose, who had been smoking steadily, didn't feel tired any more. He felt light and strong and careless. Then his back began to bristle like a hairbrush and he felt bad and mean.

"Whee-ee-ee!" he shouted suddenly and leapt up. "I'm thunder. I'm lightning. I'm a three-horned bull. Out of my way, dogs; my name is blood-drinker."

And he went out of the yard, into the lane, all taut and stiff-legged; with his eyes flickering and his teeth going click-click. Two yellow Kingston dogs came bounding up, ready to tear him, and Mongoose sniggered, like the bolt of a rifle going in and out. The dogs ran howling, their yellow hides turning grey with terror.

That night Mongoose killed forty chickens around the lane. The next night he killed eighty further afield. The third night, up in the suburbs, he killed over two hundred chickens. The next day they ran his story on the front page.

But Mongoose was only getting warmed up. He began to go into Saint Andrew, to all the doctors, police officers, lawyers and big merchants. He ravaged their chickens, their turkeys and even their dogs. He ripped the tyres of their cars and the bark of their fruit trees. Mongoose grew lean and hard as a six-inch nail and nobody knew where or when he would strike next. At night they would hear him pass on the road, his teeth going click-click, and mothers would hug their children in bed and fathers stand at the windows with loaded revolvers. They hunted him with detectives, soldiers, stool pigeons and a helicopter, but he always hid out when the hunt was on. They even sent for bloodhounds, but when he had dealt with the first one to find him the others lay down and refused to budge.

So everyone was in quite a state; and the governor, the colonial secretary, the chief justice and all the bishops offered five hundred pounds to anyone who could bring Mongoose in, dead or alive.

About this time a man named Ananias Brown came back from Panama. He was tall and dressed in a yellow suit and blue shoes, with a green tie and a pink and pearl shirt. His face was dark, beautiful and shrewd, gleaming like bronze.

"Cho," he said. "All this fuss over a Mongoose. Watch me get him. I need the money for cigarettes."

Ananias had his own way of doing things, and one morning he ran Mongoose to earth in the drainpipe where he was resting up.

"Good day, Mongoose," said Ananias. "How are you, sir?"

Mongoose click-clicked his teeth.

"Cho, man," said Ananias. "Why you click yo' teeth at me? I'm your friend. I certainly laffed when you chewed up the tyres on all those cars outside the Legislative Council."

Mongoose laughed. It sounded like a machine gun far away in the hills.

"But look here, Mongoose," continued Ananias. "I have a little proposition for you. How'd you like for them to give you all the chicken you want? Without you having to steal it?"

Mongoose said something very nasty.

"No, honest, Mongoose, man. It won't be free. You'll have to pay an entrance fee."

"How much?" asked Mongoose.

"Only two *cojones*," said Ananias.

Now Mongoose was country-bred. He'd never been to Panama or Cuba and he didn't know Spanish. But, he thought, I won't let on to that. It would never do if these people imagined I was just an ignorant, coarse bum.

"It's a deal," he said, slithering out of the pipe. "I'll have to go to the bank for those *cojones* though. I don't have that much on me."

"Why, sure you do," said Ananias. And his knife went swish.

So *that's* what *cojones* are, said Mongoose to himself. But he was already going flabby and docile, and when Ananias picked him up he didn't have the spirit even to bite. They put him in a cage at the Institute and gave him chicken and raw liver every day. He grew plump and sleek and cuddly, and everyone forgot all the trouble he had caused.

However, one little boy who came to see him one day, said sadly, "I know he killed my Daddy's chickens, and chewed the tyres off my Daddy's car, but all the same I liked him much better when he had his *cojones*."

The Bridge

They stopped the jeep about noon by the steep bank where the chestnut trees grew down to the roadside. Ian MacAlla got out first, swinging himself lithely on to the warm, dusty road from the front seat where he sat beside the sergeant who had driven them from the coast. The sergeant's name was Logan; and he and MacAlla had been together for most of the war.

"Get the lunch out," MacAlla told Sergeant Logan. "This is a good place to eat. I'll be along in a minute."

He began to walk away from the jeep, down the steep road lined with chestnuts; towards the bend in the road from where you could see the plain below.

When he had gone a little way, Sergeant Logan called after him. "I'll take the grub up under the trees, eh, sir?"

"Yes, *sir*," the sergeant said to the pink long-faced private who was picking up, in the back seat, the side pack with their rations, "that's the sort of war I like to fight. Lunch in the woods. This is a lovely way to fight a war. Come on, Horsie, let's go."

Horsie was the name the private had acquired in the short time since he had come out from England to this theatre of the war. He followed the sergeant as the man scrambled up the bank into the deeper shade of the trees. They sat down under one, leaning their backs against the trunk, and waiting for their officer.

At the bend in the road, Ian MacAlla stopped and stood with his legs slightly apart, his head bent a little forward. He took off the floppy-crowned, peaked cap and let the small mountain breeze blow across his fair, bleached hair. The war had not troubled this part of the country much. There had been a lot of fighting at the sea, and for a little way inland. And now farther up among the mountains, near the passes, there was more fighting. But from where he stood there was almost no destruction to see.

Hardly any sign, even, of military activity except for a few trucks on the plain below which were driving up to the front.

Across the plain the road was cast in a clean straight line.

It ran between pale-green, undulating sweeps of corn, dark rows of orange and tightly rolled columns of cypress. The houses on the plain were, from where he stood, distinct small cubes with red roofs and flamboyant sides. Each village and cluster of houses was set amid fruit trees and shade trees.

When the road reached the foothills it suddenly began to coil and twist under the stress of the mountains. It vanished and reappeared endlessly among the drab green of the olive groves and brighter, precise vineyards. There was a broad valley on his left with vineyards up the sides. And far away behind his right hand were hazy blue peaks. That was where the fighting was.

Far down on the flat land, just beyond a village, was an abandoned half-track lying on its side, half in, half out of the ditch beside the white road. Here and there among the green and the rocks of the hillsides there were dug-outs and machine-gun emplacements that had never been used because the war had gone through this place so quickly.

MacAlla stood quite still at the bend in the road, filling himself carefully with the country that surrounded him. He had not seen this place for nearly five years. Not since the year before the war, but before that he used to come to it often. He had been very much afraid, during all the years he was fighting his way towards it, that this country he loved and knew so well had been destroyed, burnt up and broken like all the other countries and places he had passed through. And then this morning, when he had driven up from the coast and seen how much the land had been spared, something in his stomach had slowly, warmly and pleasantly relaxed. As they had climbed the mountain road and he had seen the men and the women working among the vines he had come to feel a sense of gratitude far stronger than his fear of going back to the war.

He stretched himself happily in the hot mountain sun, took three great breaths of pure excitement, then turned and walked quickly back to where the sergeant and the private sat under the chestnut trees. Beside the hard rations of biscuit and tinned beef they had two kilos of peaches which he had bought earlier in the morning down on the plain. He had also bought two bottles of red wine and three of those thick little tumblers you get in the cheaper wine shops. By the time they had reached the fruit he was a little drunk with the wine, and with the happiness of coming back to this antique, indestructible country, and finding so much of it the same and undestroyed.

He looked at the dark, tight face of Sergeant Logan and the pink, long face of the young private who had not been in any of the fighting yet. He wanted, very much, to tell them what this day and this place meant to him. But he did not try because he knew his feeling and his happiness was the sum of too many things. It was the magical and delicate addition of the wine and the big bronze peaches which they dipped into the wine between each bite. Also, it was the hard graceful landscape, and the three-thousand-year habits of farming and husbandry the people were practising among the olives and the vineyards. It was the pale, very clear sky shifting behind the restless leaves. For him, too, it had the flavour and memory of a great many books, poems and works of art which he did not think the others would be able to share. But all through the meal, which was eaten in silence, he had a tight urgent pressure in his chest to share his experience. To show them the promise and endurance and the goodness that lay about them.

After he had finished his wine he got up and went down to the jeep. He sat on the fender, leaning his elbow on the bonnet and smoking a cigarette. In a little while, as he had hoped, Sergeant Logan came over to him and he offered him a cigarette. They smoked quietly, but with no constraint in their silence. The sergeant was leaning his forearms on the side of the jeep, and frowning in a worried way at the hazy blue peaks where the fighting was, where they were going.

"This is a pretty good country, eh?" MacAlla asked the sergeant.

"Yes," the sergeant said, "it's a nice country, sir. Have you been here before?"

"Oh, yes," MacAlla told him. "Before the war I used to come here quite a lot. I generally stayed at a little village a bit up the road. You wait till you see that village, sergeant. It's damn near perfect. It has everything a man should have in his community. After this war is over I'm going back there for two months, until I start thinking properly about things again."

Sitting there on the jeep in the hot mountain sun, with the cool wind on him, he found it very easy to remember the village, and the bridge that led across the ravine and joined it to the road on the other side. He could see it exactly as it had been the first time.

It had been his first time abroad. He had come walking up this same road one very hot summer's day. The air had been full of the noise of bees and of the torrent further up the mountain sounding through the leaves. He had come to the village late in the afternoon. The roar of the torrent was louder and the afternoon light was hard as a diamond. By now, pines as well as chestnuts grew on the mountain slopes. Everything had been cool and subtly exciting, as if he were walking on the floor of a still, transparent lake.

The village when he came to it had been suddenly and beautifully carved against the mountain. Houses built on outcrops of rocks, or on platforms cut into the earth. The church on a round pinnacle, higher than the rest, with the cross against the deep sky, above the trees. Everything was softer and deeper in tone than it was on the plain. Only a few people to be seen, walking in a steady, unlanguid rhythm. When he had passed them, on the cobbled street under the grey walls, they looked at him with friendly curiosity.

He had not meant to stop that day in the village, however, until he saw the bridge. But it had been the bridge which made the village, and the bridge together with the village symbolized a pattern he had wanted to find for a long time, perhaps without knowing it.

He had kept on walking through the village, along the road and round the small spur that butted over the ravine. And here, as he had seen the bridge, he suddenly stopped. He had stopped as though a huge and invisible fist had been suddenly flung into his face. For a long time that day he remained there, letting the first sight of the bridge come to him, not wanting to spoil the surprise of it all. He had learnt, then, for the first time, that everyone has his private vulnerable moment.

And now, thought Ian MacAlla, here I am, sitting on the fender of a jeep, in the middle of a war which I have disliked as much as I've ever disliked anything: and that bridge is going to be there, just because some kind fate decided to save this particular corner of sanity alive. He grinned suddenly at Logan; the man grinned back, full of understanding. And MacAlla tried to tell him something about the bridge.

He told him about the columns plunging fifty feet down from the span into the bed of the torrent; and the arches leaping across the ravine in small, lovely sweeps. How the stones had weathered for over one thousand years into a warm golden surface that seemed, when you touched it, to quiver faintly like the hide of some perfectly magnificent animal. He also tried to tell him, but he was less successful, how, in the afternoons, the mountain hung its shadow across the road; how the axes of the charcoal burners rang lazily down the mountain side; and how the voices of the women in the ravine, as they squatted over their washing at the torrent's edge, drifted up like smoke on the golden air; and of the road on the other side, winding like a ragged scar among the dark life of the trees. As they talked the faces of the two men became relaxed and full of confidence. They had been very close to each other on several occasions in the past few years, but this afternoon was the day they began to know each other really well.

After a while, when they had run out of things to say and had smoked another cigarette, MacAlla jumped off the fender into the old dust of the road.

"Ah well," he said, "let's go. Back to the bloody war."

"Yes, sir," said the sergeant. His face was not relaxed or confident any more. "Come on, Horsie," he shouted to the private. "Mind your kidneys, sleeping in the damp."

The private jumped up and came trotting down the bank, rubbing his eyes and yawning. He flung the side pack which had contained their rations into the seat. He got in, still sleepy, and wedged himself in the corner. MacAlla climbed in beside Logan in the front seat, and the sergeant put the jeep into gear and drove off.

All the way up the mountain road, coming to the village, MacAlla was silent, happy and nervous with anticipation. The chestnuts and pines stood as he remembered them, dark, cool, full of excitement and promise. Only the road had been damaged – rutted by the trucks and tanks of two armies.

"We'll get to the village in about five minutes," he told Logan when they had been driving for about half an hour.

The sergeant was easing the jeep around a steep hairpin; he changed down, then as the wheels bit into the road and the engine caught on to the grade he turned to MacAlla and smiled very kindly.

"You want to stop in the village?" he asked. "Do you have any friends there you want to see?"

"Yes," MacAlla told him, "I used to have quite a few friends there. I'm almost afraid to stop and ask how many are left, though. But I want to go on to the bridge first, I'd like to see that before anything." He wondered if the people in the village, whom he had known before the war, would remember him, or recognize him now.

The village was all right, it hadn't been touched at all. The first thing he saw was the cross against the sky, above the trees. Then the rest of the houses, set hard and secure against the mountain. There was hardly anyone in the streets; only a little boy leading a goat who drew aside and waved casually.

MacAlla leant out of the jeep slightly looking ahead along the road.

Going round the small spur that butted over the ravine where the bridge was, he foreknew something was going to be wrong. It came to him without warning, in a sudden, freezing breath. All at once he realized that on the other side of the spur he was going to take a beating, and he began to prepare for it.

He sat impassively as the sergeant spun the jeep round the spur and eased the vehicle over the massive iron planks of the military bridge that now crossed the ravine. MacAlla let the broken stumps of masonry, which were left from the old bridge, register on his mind. He felt perfectly blank and hollow. When they reached the other side he said to Logan,

"Stop the car."

His voice was steady and officer-crisp; but there was an emptiness in his chest and stomach.

He climbed out of the jeep and walked down the road to the new bridge.

When he got out of earshot the private said, "What's hit the old man, Sarge? He looks as if a ghost had kissed him."

The sergeant let this go without answering. He did not even turn his head.

When MacAlla reached the pile of iron that had been flung across the ravine, he finally saw what had happened to the old bridge. It lay at the bottom of the shallow brown torrent in shattered heaps. Among the pieces was the huge, gaunt, German tank that had finally shaken the arch stones out and gone through to the bottom. The German engineers, he decided, must have blown up the rest of it to build the iron bridge. One side of him wondered why they hadn't dismantled it when they had crossed; he decided it must have been because they went through in such a hell of a hurry.

It was a good job they had done, he decided, as his boots clanged distantly and mournfully on the iron planks of the bridge. This one should last nearly a fifth as long as the old one if it wasn't pulled down and replaced. Yes, he told himself, and slapped his heel down hard on the iron, a really good professional job.

He walked across it and on the other side turned down the little path that led to the women's washing place at the bottom of the ravine. He could hear their voices now. Halfway down the path he stopped. He looked at the squatting outline of the bridge and at the tank with its huge cannon pointing forlornly to the sky, the brown-green water of the torrent swirling round its tracks.

"Oh, hell," said MacAlla. "Wouldn't you just know it."

He went back up the path, across the bridge to the road where Logan had parked the jeep. He didn't want to see anyone in the village just now. The numbness and the sickness were wearing off; but there was a sterile, nasty taste of anger and impotence at the back of his throat. Also, he did not think what that bridge had represented could be replaced by his generation, and it was a very sad and bitter thing to know.

He got to the jeep and scrambled in again beside Logan.

"Let's go straight on," he said, "I'll come back later."

"Yes, sir," said Sergeant Logan, and started the engine.

Then, "I'm sorry about your bridge," said the sergeant.

"That's all right, sergeant," MacAlla told him. "It wasn't my goddam bridge anyway."

A Village Tragedy

The old boar slashed Ambrose Beckett across the abdomen. It was done between one brazen squeal and another, while Ambrose Beckett still turned on the wet clay of the path and before the echo of his last, useless shot wandered among the big peaks around the valley.

The men with whom Ambrose Beckett had been hunting turned and saw the ridge-backed, red-bristled beast vanish like a cannon ball into a long stretch of fairy bamboo, which can cling like cobwebs and cut like broken glass if you are a man and not a pig who has been hunted for five years, has killed fourteen dogs, and just killed its first man. Before the men reached him, they saw Ambrose Beckett's wildly unbelieving face, like grey stone, and the dark arches of his spurting blood shining on the wet dull clay under the tree ferns. Then he had fallen like a wet towel among the leaf mould, clutching the clay in his slack fingers, with one distant, protesting scream sounding from the back of his throat.

They bandaged him, after stuffing, inexpertly, bits of their shirts and handkerchiefs into his wounds. Nothing they did, however, could stop a fast, thick welling of blood from where he had been torn. And no comfort could stop his strangled, far-away screaming. They made some sort of a stretcher from two green branches and a blanket. They covered him with another blanket and began to carry him across the mountains to the village. The trail was very narrow and the floor of the rain forest was steep and wet. Each time they slipped and recovered balance, they jolted the stretcher.

After a while they forced themselves not to shudder as Ambrose Beckett screamed. Soon he began to moan and the slow, dirty blood began to trickle from his mouth, and they knew that he would never reach the village alive.

When they realized this, they decided to send Mass Ken's half-witted son, Joseph, ahead of them to tell the doctor and the parson. Joseph was the biggest idiot any man could remember being born in the village. He inhabited a world of half-articulate fantasy and ridiculous confusion. He was strong enough to kill a man with his hands, and he wept if a child frowned at him. In Cayuna the children do not throw stones at their naturals, but they tease them, and Joseph, who loved to wait outside the school and watch the children going home, would be seen crouched between the roots of the cotton tree, weeping disconsolately because the boys had scowled as they passed and said: "Joseph! What you doin' here, man?" He could learn nothing, and remembered little from one minute to the next unless you dealt him a blow across the head when giving him the simplest instructions. But he was marvellous on the mountains: tireless as a mule and much faster.

Now, with Ambrose Beckett dying on the blanket, the men standing around gave Joseph his instructions. "Doctor!" said Mass Ken, his father, and cuffed Joseph across his slab of a head. "Doctor! You hear?" He hit him again. "Tell doctor an' tell parson dem mus' come quick. Tell dem come quick, you hear! Tell dem Mass Ambrose sick bad. Sick! Sick! You hear!" Joseph's big, stone head rocked again under a blow, and his odd, disorganized face closed its askew planes into a grin of pure understanding. He went off among the huge trees and thick wet bush and into the mist. When he had gone ten steps they could no longer hear him.

It was twelve miles and four thousand feet down to the village and he did it in four hours. At ten o'clock that night he started to bang happily on the door of the manse, and kept it up until the Reverend Mackinnon put his head out of the window. When he heard the shutter slamming against the wall, Joseph ran to the middle of the lawn, capering and shouting.

"What?" called the Reverend Mackinnon. "What is it, Joseph?"

He could see nothing but a vague, starlit blur bounding up and down the lawn, but he recognized the manner and the voice. Joseph jumped higher and shouted again, his voice tight and brazen with self-importance.

Finally the Reverend Mackinnon came downstairs and, when Joseph ran to the door, cuffed the boy until he became calm. Then he got the story.

"Doctor!" he said, turning Joseph around and giving him a push. Leaving the parson, Joseph ran across the damp Bahama grass of the lawn to where he could see the deep yellow of a light in one window of a big house along the road. Doctor Rushie was still up: it was one of the nights that he got drunk, as he did, regularly and alone, twenty times a month.

"Good God!" said Rushie. "How far up did it happen, Joseph?"

Joseph gestured. Distance, except in terms of feet and yards, was not of much importance in his life.

"Have you told parson?" the doctor asked. He was drunk, but not much. Had the news come a little later, he would have been very drunk and quite incapable. He went to the window and bawled for his servant. "Saddle the mule," Doctor Rushie shouted, "and put on your clothes. Bring a lantern. Hurry up!"

In about five minutes the doctor was riding out of the village, with his manservant trotting ahead, the circle of light from the lantern sliding quickly from side to side across the path. There was a stand of golden-cup trees along this stretch of the bridle path and the dropped fruit broke wetly under the hooves of the mule and a thick, sugary scent came up on the cold air cutting through the hot, oily smell of the lantern.

They overtook the Reverend Mackinnon, who had no manservant and who was riding his stubby, grey gelding alone in the dark. By the lantern light, Doctor Rushie could see the parson's very pale, long face and his lank grey hair fallen across his forehead and full of burrs from the long grass of the steep bank beside the narrow path.

"You've heard?" the doctor said. It was not really a question and they were riding on in the darkness behind the bob and sway of the lantern while the parson was nodding his head.

Back on the road, Joseph sat on a big stone outside the doctor's house. Nobody had told him what to do after delivering his messages and he felt confused and restless. The doctor's house, and the Reverend Mackinnon's, were up the road from the village. Neither man had thought to inform people down there as to what had happened up on the mountain. Soon

Joseph rose from the stone, ran down the road to the village and began to race about the street from side to side, talking loudly to himself. It was not long before he had awakened every house within sound of his voice.

"Joseph, you bad boy," screeched Mr Tennant, the schoolmaster. "What are you doing here? At this hour." Joseph flapped a big dirty hand at him excitedly. "Boy, if I bring a switch out to you . . ." Mr Tennant said. Joseph shot away down the street like a dog, but he continued to talk very loudly.

Mr Tennant, with a tight, moist smile on his plump lips and carrying a long supplejack cane, came from his house. Joseph bolted for the shoemaker's doorway. Only Elvira, Joseph's smallest sister, could get as much sense from his clogged speech as quickly as Mass Emmanuel, the shoemaker.

"Joseph," said Mass Emmanuel, as the natural found refuge in his doorway, "why you not sleepin', eh? What a bad bwoy. I've a good mind to let teacher flog you."

He put an arm across the boy's trembling shoulders and drew him close.

Joseph told him about Ambrose Beckett, imitating with great vividness the terrible, ripping twitch of the boar's head writhing enthusiastically on the ground to show what it had been like with Mass Ambrose. Mass Emmanuel translated as the people began to come from the houses. Then they all looked up to the hill at the other end of the village, to where Ambrose Beckett's house stood. They began to move towards the house.

"Lawd King!" said Miss Vera Brownford. "Fancy! Mass Ambrose! A fine man like dat. Poor Miss Louise!"

She was the centre of the older women of the village as they went up the hill to the house where Ambrose and Louise Beckett had lived for thirty years. Vera Brownford was ninety-eight, or maybe a hundred. Perhaps she was much more. Her first grandchild had been born before anyone now alive in the village, and only a few people could still remember her, dimly, in early middle age. Her intimate participation in every birth, death and wedding was, for the village, an obligatory ritual. She had lived so long and so completely that she had grown to want nothing except freedom from pain. At times the shadow-line between life and death was not very distinct to her expectation, her desire or her feeling but she understood the terror and confusion that the crossing of the line brought to those younger than herself. And, understanding this, she gave comfort as a tree gives shade, or as a stream gives water to those who fetch it, with a vast, experienced impartiality. It was her occupation.

Among the younger men and women Joseph was still the centre of interest as they went up the hill. His mime performance of Ambrose Beckett and the boar had begun to acquire the finish of art. In all his life he had never experienced such respect for his ability and knowledge. He was almost gone off his poor mind with happiness.

"Joseph," said Mass Emmanuel suddenly, coming back down the path which was leading them to Louise Beckett's darkened house. "Joseph. I forgot. We gwine to need ice to pack Mass Ambrose. Tell dem to give you ice. Ice, you hear. At Irish Corner."

He gave a five-shilling note to the boy and hugged the huge, smoothly sloping shoulders and smiled at him. Only for two people, Elvira and Emmanuel, would Joseph remember anything unaccompanied by a blow.

Joseph turned and raced down the path. He seemed to weave through the murmurous crowd like a twist of smoke. Before he was out of earshot they heard him singing his own chant, which was a mingle of all the hymns and songs he had ever listened to. He was always adding to it, and though it had no more conscious structure than a roll of thunder, it had a remarkable, pervasive quality, coming to you from a dozen points at once, with odd limping echoes.

The Reverend Mackinnon and Doctor Rushie met the party of returning hunters about five miles from the village. They heard the dogs barking and saw the lantern lights jump among the pines on the saddle between the peaks ahead of them. This was on the side of a great valley, on a trail worn through a stretch of ginger lilies. The night was very cold and mist was coming down from the sharp, fuzzy peaks and piling into the valley below, and the air was full of a thin, spicy tang as the hooves crushed the long ginger-lily leaves against the stones.

"Ho-yah!" shouted the doctor's manservant when they saw the lights. "Is dat you, Mass Ken?"

"Yes." The answer rolled back slowly, thin and lost in the air of the huge valley. "Who dere?"

"Doctor. Doctor and parson. How Mass Ambrose stay?"

"Him dead!"

He was dead, right enough, when the two parties met. In the glare from the lanterns his skin was the colour of dough and earth mixed, quite drained of blood. The blankets between which he lay were dark and odorous with blood. His mouth had half opened and one eye had closed tightly, twisting his face and leaving the other eye open. It gave him an unbelievably knowing and cynical leer.

"Well, I'll be damned," Doctor Rushie said. And then, seeing Mackinnon's face, "Beg your pardon; but look at that."

"Look at what?" the Reverend Mackinnon said stiffly. He had never liked Rushie much, and now he did not like him at all.

"His face. How many dead men have you seen?"

"I don't know. As many as you, I suppose."

"Exactly," Doctor Rushie said. "Probably more. But how many have you seen die with one eye closed? You know it's generally both eyes wide open. Sometimes both closed, but not often. Damned odd, eh?"

"I hardly think it's important, doctor," the Reverend Mackinnon said. His long, ugly, Scots face was tightly ridged with disgust. Only the presence of the villagers kept him polite.

"No," the doctor said, "it's not important. I just noticed it. Well, no point in hanging around here. Let's get him home, eh?"

Going down the track, the doctor and the parson rode behind.

"What a dreadful thing to have happened, eh, doctor?" said the Reverend Mackinnon. "I can hardly believe it."

He always felt guilty about not liking Doctor Rushie; and he constantly asked himself wherein he as a minister had failed to contact the drunken, savagely isolated creature who rode behind him.

"I can believe it," the doctor said. "Do you know how many ways the world has of killing you? I was adding up the other night. It comes to thousands. Simply thousands."

The Reverend Mackinnon could find no answer to this. There were answers, he knew, but none that he cared to risk with the lonely, brutal man who, more or less, cared for the health of their village and a score of other villages in the district.

He's not even a very good doctor, the Reverend Mackinnon thought, and felt a cold flush of shame because the thought gave him satisfaction.

"He was such a strong, vital man, too," the Reverend Mackinnon said a little later. He was unable to bear the night with the mist blowing damp and cold across his face, piling up in the valley so that it seemed they were riding across the air, and the bobbing lanterns lighting up the silent men as they scrambled awkwardly with the stretcher on the narrow track.

"He was a strong man," the doctor said dryly.

"Why, the other day I saw him clearing that land of his up by the river, with his two sons. He was doing twice as much as they," Mackinnon continued.

"Oh, he was a good farmer, all right," the doctor agreed, in the same dry tone. "He ought to have been, with what he had acquired these last few years. He knew what he wanted, all right."

"He was an example to his community," Mackinnon said with solemn emphasis. "God-fearing and responsible. An example. If only he'd had an education. They would have made him a justice of the peace. He was an example. A Christian example."

"Well, maybe the boys will become examples, too," the doctor told him.

"The boys," said Reverend Mackinnon, "the boys have fallen far from the stem. Thomas has his father's sense of duty, but he is weak. And Sidney cares only for himself, his pleasures and his land. He caused Ambrose Beckett a great deal of worry. Which one of them do you think will get the holding, eh? Thomas or Sidney?"

"Couldn't say," the doctor replied. "I was only Beckett's doctor not his lawyer. Probably they'll have equal shares. He had enough, God knows, for these parts."

The Reverend Mackinnon frowned and shifted uneasily in the saddle. *Oh God,* he said to himself, *make Thomas get the holding.* He looked sombrely over the nodding head of his beast and at the vague blur of the stretcher. The men were moving fast now, because Ambrose Beckett was dead and they could heave the stretcher about quickly.

Twenty years before this, Ambrose Beckett had rented land from the church. It was the first move in a programme which had made him the largest peasant farmer in the parish. It had been good land and he had paid a good rent. But since the war, when everything had gone up, the rent had fallen to a fraction of the land's value, and the Reverend Mackinnon had been looking for some way to increase it. He was, essentially, a timid man who only felt courage and confidence on Sunday, when he stood unassailable in the pulpit, beyond interruption, with God and the Hosts at his back.

His method of attack in the matter of the rent had been to mount a series of hints. Veiled and off-hand at first, they had evolved, after three years, into frequent references about the difficulties and embarrassments of a priest in the modern world. Pride and timidity had kept him from stating an open claim. These and the reasonable certainty that Ambrose Beckett would, at first, refuse to pay more. Would refuse with the plausibility and righteousness of a man who valued an acre, really, more than he regarded a wife, and who knew his own usefulness as a parishioner.

I am not covetous, the Reverend Mackinnon told himself in the darkness. *I do not want it for myself. But the manse is falling to bits and if I send Jean home next year she will need clothes. Perhaps two sets within the year; girls grow so fast at her age.*

Given time, he knew, he could have persuaded Ambrose Beckett. It would have been painful, but it would have come. Now he would have to begin again with the sons. If Thomas were the heir, it would be easy. He was a gentle, almost girlish lad, very devout and proud of his family's influence in the church. But Sidney. Sidney would be difficult. Difficult and slow. And arrogant. He had always treated the Reverend Mackinnon with a casual politeness more infuriating than hostility. A bland indifference which only on occasion became genially ferocious. The afternoon, for instance, when Mackinnon had caught him making love to a little East Indian girl under a huge rock by the river. The lad had raised his head from beside the girl's blind, contorted face and stared at the parson with cool, amused malice. And the next day, Sunday, while Mackinnon was preaching a sermon on the sin of fornication, he had looked down from the pulpit to the front pew where Ambrose Beckett sat in a hot, high-buttoned black suit among his family, and had seen such a sparkle of conspiratorial intimacy in Sidney's eyes that he had floundered in his speech.

While they were bringing the body of Ambrose Beckett down from the mountain, Joseph had reached the market town of Irish Corner. He knocked on the zinc fence around the shop until the Chinese keeper came down and a small crowd had gathered. Then he told the story of Ambrose and the boar again, giving a really practised and gigantic performance. He had great difficulty in making them understand what had happened, or what he wanted, but they finally got it. Then they cut a great block of ice, wrapped it in a crocus bag, hoisted it on to Joseph's head, and set him on the road back to the village.

He had hardly stopped running since the late afternoon and he streamed with sweat as if he had been put under a hose; but he was not tired and he was crazy with excitement. He had never played such a central part in anything before.

Suddenly he slowed his long, effortless jog-trot up the steep road. He stopped. The ice in its wrapping of crocus bag was cool and wet between his hands and on his huge, idol's head. From his great heaving lungs there burst an ecstatic grunt. Ice . . . ice . . . *ice.* If he got back quickly, they would chip a white, glittering, jagged lump for him; a piece around which he could curl his tongue. A bit to hold above his opened mouth, so that the cold, unimaginable drops would hit the back of his throat. A bit with edges he could rub across tightly shut eyelids and then feel the cold water drying on his skin. He danced with happiness, balancing the huge block as if it were a hat. As far up as his village, ice was still a luxury for all but the doctor, who had a machine which made ice-cubes.

The people at Ambrose Beckett's house heard the dogs as the men came up the hill. Louise Beckett rushed from the house and down the path towards the light from the lanterns. When she saw the stretcher she began to cry and moan wildly, covering her face and clutching her body. Her two sons came close to her.

"Mother . . . Mother," Thomas said. He embraced her tightly and began to cry, too.

Sidney put his arm around her shoulder and said softly: "I will take care of you, mother. I will take care of you. Don't cry. Don't cry."

Inside the house, the body was laid out on the kitchen table. The table was too short and the feet hung over the edge. Doctor Rushie shut the people out and by the light of four lamps sewed up the hideous openings in

Ambrose Beckett's body. Once during this operation he spoke, as if to the corpse. "You poor devil," he said, "this must have hurt like blazes. But the other thing would have hurt you more and it would have lasted longer."

Outside, in the tiny, stiffly furnished drawing room, Vera Brown-ford sat on the old-fashioned horsehair sofa. Louise Beckett sat close up beside her, resting her head on that old, indestructible breast which was as thin and hard as a piece of hose-pipe, and yet as hugely comfortable as a warm ocean.

"Cry good, child," Vera Brownford said. "Cry good. If you don't cry you will get sick. Oh, Lawd, it hard to lose a man. It hard to lose a good man like Ambrose. Cry good, child. It much easier."

The old, dry voice flowed smoothly, uttering banalities that sheer experience gave the weight of poetry. Louise Beckett cried noisily.

The women of the village stood around the sofa; the men gathered near the door and outside, each group around one of the hunters, who told in whispers what it had been like. The children waited on the fringes of each group, some of them looking with wide stares towards the locked kitchen door.

The Reverend Mackinnon hovered between the men and the women. Finally he went across to Louise Beckett.

"Louise," he said, "you must take comfort. Remember that your beloved husband is not gone. He only waits for you in our Master's house. He was a good man, Louise. A true Christian man. Take comfort in that, and in the promise of everlasting life."

Louise Beckett raised her stunned face and looked at him from red eyes. "Thank you, parson," she whispered, and burrowed her head against Vera Brownford's breast.

Among the men, Huntley was saying in a hard, unbelieving voice: "Jesus, it happen so quick. I tell you, Mass Emmanuel, it happen before we even see it."

"How things happen so, eh?" Emmanuel said. "Truly, it is like the Bible say: in the midst of life we are in death."

"That is true, Emmanuel," said the Reverend Mackinnon, joining them. "That is very true." He laid a hand on Sidney's shoulder and gave it a little squeeze. "But remember, as Christians we need not fear death if we live so that death finds us prepared for God. We must remember the life God showed us through His only Son and, in our turn, live so that each day we can say to ourselves: Today I did God's will."

He looked closely at Sidney as he spoke; but the young man's face was closed, sullen with grief and unreadable.

Mr Tennant, the schoolmaster, cleared his throat. He thought very highly of the Reverend Mackinnon, but he also felt that, in the village, he should reinforce the parson. Provide the practical epilogues to the more refined utterances of the church.

"It is you and Thomas now, Sidney," Mr Tennant said. "You must act like men. Work the land as diligently as your father. Look after your good mother . . ."

They heard a hard, heavy grunting outside in the dark, and then Joseph stepped into the room. He was lathered about the lips, with sweat and water from the ice mingled on his face and staining his clothes. Everyone stopped talking when they saw the ice.

Mass Ken, Joseph's father, took the boy by the arm and led him into the bedroom. Four of the men who had hunted that day with Ambrose Beckett followed him. They stripped the clothes and mattress from the springs and spread old newspapers under the bed. They unwrapped the ice from the coarse, shaggy crocus and one of the men split it into five great lumps with an ice pick. Then they spread old newspapers on the bare springs and waited awkwardly in the half-dark of the little bedroom where Ambrose Beckett had lain with his wife for thirty years.

Outside, one of the younger men who had been on the hunt laid his hand shyly on Sidney's arm.

"Sidney," he said, "I sorry, you see. If it was me own Papa, I couldn't sorry more. Lawd, Sidney, don't worry. I will help you. You gwine need anoder man to help you wid dat lan' you an' Mass Ambrose was clearing? What you gwine put in it, bwoy? It is one nice piece of ground."

Tears shone in Sidney's eyes. He was remembering how powerful and comforting his father had looked in the sunlight as they cleared the land by the river. His friend's words were sweet and warm and made him feel comforted again.

"T'ank you, Zack," he said. "T'ank you. Thomas an' me will need a help.

Papa did want to put citrus in dat piece. Dat is de crop pay well now, you know. Since de war over, everybody want orange oil again."

Thomas looked suddenly and with disturbance at his brother.

"When Papa say we was gwine put citrus in?" he asked. "You know we only talk about it. Las' time we talk, you remember I say we should plant ginger. I like ginger. It safe."

"Everybody plant ginger, Thomas," Sidney said gently and inflexibly. "Papa did always say too much ginger was gwine to kill de smallholders. Time some of us plant somet'ing else."

The door to the kitchen opened and they saw Doctor Rushie framed in the opening, with the lamplight yellow behind him. Sidney and Thomas, Mass Ken and Emmanuel went into the kitchen and brought the body out. Some of the women began to wail. Louise Beckett set up a long howling cry and ran across the room. She held the dead face between her hands. She was twitching like an exhausted animal.

"Mass Ambrose," she cried, "Mass Ambrose."

After they had packed the body among the ice lumps, the Reverend Mackinnon led them in prayer around the bed. Then the people started to go home. All went except Vera Brownford and three of Louise Beckett's closest friends, who stayed to watch the body.

It was now the blackest part of the morning, before the sun began to touch the mountain tops and make the sky glow with pink and green.

The Reverend Mackinnon went home and tiredly unsaddled his stumpy grey gelding. He went up to bed and thought about the gentle, exhausted wife he had buried two years before, and worried about the plump, soundly sleeping daughter a hundred miles away in boarding school.

Doctor Rushie went home, and his manservant led the mule away while the doctor sat down to finish the bottle he had been drinking when Joseph came. He thought about the wounds in Ambrose Beckett's body and whether, if he had got to him right away, he could have saved a life. He thought, also, about the sliver from Ambrose Beckett's rectum which he had sent down to Queenshaven for analysis a week ago and which, he was sure, showed the beginnings of cancer.

Lying in the bed they had shared from childhood, Sidney and Thomas clung to each other and sobbed in the painful, tearing manner of grown men. In between grieving for their father, they argued fiercely and quietly as to the wisdom of planting citrus or ginger.

In the room with the body, the women sat and watched. Once Louise Beckett leaned forward and touched the damp sheet wonderingly.

"Mass Ambrose?" she asked softly, "You gawn? You really gawn?"

In the kitchen of his home, Joseph snuggled into bed beside Elvira, his little sister, and began to cry bitterly. She woke when she heard him crying and asked him what was the matter. He told her how he had run all the way to Irish Corner and back with the ice, and how no one had thought to give him a little piece. The ingratitude and thoughtlessness of the mourners shocked the little girl profoundly. She wiped the tears from his big sweaty face and hugged him, rocking him in her thin arms and kissing him with little quick maternal pecks.

Very soon he was fast asleep.

Morning, Noon and Night

This was the hour of the day, before his morning meal, when the small desperation of his life was heaviest on his stomach. It was the time when the optimism that seemed to strengthen in the heat of the day was quite absent. Today, he told himself savagely, I gwine to get a job. Jesus Christ strike me if I don' get a job.

He pulled on his trousers and went out of the room, down the three rough-set concrete steps, to the yard. His wife Lyn was washing at the pipe; she stood with her feet apart, leaning over so the water would not splash her dress. He waited his turn among the people from the house. Yawning and stretching in the grey and pink gloom of the warm morning.

When he got back to the room she had mixed the brown sugar and water in the two enamel mugs and laid out the two penny loaves on the small newspaper-covered table. They ate in silence; quickly and concentratedly, hardly dropping a crumb of the firm thick-textured bread. Then she went out because she had to be at work by half-past six, up in the suburbs, under the hills six miles away, the house where she was the cook.

Left alone, he slouched in the straight hard chair that with the other chair, the table, and the bed was all the furniture in the small dark-brown-painted room. He reached round and took a half-smoked cigarette and a full one from the breast pocket of the shirt hanging on the chair. He looked at them for a little while, tilting his palm slightly to make them roll; then with an air of defiance and decision he put the whole cigarette in his mouth and dropped the stubbed butt back into the shirt pocket. He fumbled in his trousers for matches; and with the first slow deep draught of tobacco he felt the hope coming back to him, slowly coursing his body with the blood. I will get work today, he told himself, or somet'ing happen. Luck mus' break my way sometime.

He got up and bent for his shoes under the bed. They were black, carefully kept, neat shoes. So long a man have a good pair of shoes, him don' touch bottom yet.

About half past twelve, when the people began to come out of the offices for lunch, Reuben felt the optimism of the morning drain from him. He knew he was not going to get the job he wanted today. Not even weighing the great logs of lignum vitae as they came into the warehouses from the country trucks. That was a job he got sometimes for a day or two. One time there was a big shipment and he worked for two weeks; he earned big money that fortnight. They paid you by however much you weighed and stacked. And you could make twenty shillings a day doing it. But it was irregular, chance work; and when you hadn't been eating well for three or four weeks you soon got tired and had to slow up.

Sometimes at the end of a day your knees buckled and you had to lean your forehead on the back of the truck, holding on. Sweat ran off you as if you had been hosed down. And the beating of the heart in your breast was like a man kicking you steadily in the ribs.

When the lunch hour came, Reuben left the waterfront. He walked slowly uptown, past the big stores, to the Captain's Bar. He stood outside the bar and looked at the people coming down the sidewalk. He was waiting for one face, so he hardly saw the others except to know none of them belonging to the man he was waiting for.

While he was looking up the street a man came up behind him. The man walked with a loose springy animal stride; very fast, like a big dog loping. His thin, dark-brown face was a result of all the races that had ever come to the West Indies. It was a clever feverishly alert face. He had red-streaked soupy, drinker's eyes and his thin heavy-veined hands carried frequently a cigarette to his lips; he hardly inhaled before he jerked the cigarette away. He carried an old pigskin briefcase with faded initials, "G.K.H.".

"Hello, Reuben," he said. "Waiting for me?"

Reuben turned sharply, a curious, pleading, guilty grin forming on his face.

"Lawd, Mister Gerald, you frighten me, sah. How you do, sah?"

"All right," said Gerald Hayes the lawyer. "I'm all right, Reuben, how are you? How is Lyn?"

"Well t'ank you, sah. I is well, please God, an' so is she. I glad to see you lookin' so well, Mister Gerald."

Gerald Hayes said quickly, "Have you got a job yet, Reuben?"

"No, sah."

"I've been trying for you," Gerald told him. "But I can't say I've found anything yet."

"Lawd, Mister Gerald, sah," Reuben said, "I know you try. I know you is one man will do a t'ing if you say. you will do a t'ing."

Gerald Hayes put his hand in his pocket and brought out a half-crown piece. He pressed it into Reuben's limp hand with a practised gesture, full of pain and impotence.

He said, "God Almighty, Reuben, I wish I could find you something. I wish I could find every son of a bitch in this goddam island something to do. I wish to God a lusty brute like you didn't have to wait on me outside this bloody rumshop for a handout. I wish I didn't have you on my conscience; then maybe I'd be able to really enjoy life and all the goddam money I keep on making."

Reuben let all this go in and out of his ears without it really touching his brain. He knew Gerald Hayes was not speaking to him, but to some castrated, half-dead vision from a long time ago. He had known Hayes for a great number of years; from the time when he had been yard boy for Hayes's father and mother. They were both about fourteen in those days.

He smiled again; this time without the guilt. He said, with enormous gentleness, "Cho, Mister Gerald, you don' have to feel like dat."

A tall, very fair Englishman passed them and laid one hand on the swinging door of the bar. He said over his shoulder in a voice as cool and groomed as his clothes, "Coming in, Gerald?"

"Be right with you, Arthur," said Gerald Hayes. "Set up for me, will you."

He put his hand on Reuben's shoulder and pressed it hard. He turned into the bar.

Reuben went back to the warehouses on the waterfront. Along Port Royal Street the heat steamed the sugar and rum and spice smell out of the iron-shuttered warehouses: the day was lazy and loud with flies and bees: the palms were green and still in the bright air above the offices of the Caribbean Trading Company carved against the hard flat sky. The yellow-beaked crows, with their raw red heads and rusty black bodies, wheeled casually above the glistening zinc roofs. The noon-hour heaviness lay across the dirt-dusted street: between the shafts of the huge flour-dusted drays the mules hung their great heads and dozed.

The old woman who sold patties was squatted against one of the warehouse walls on her little stool. He went up and asked for two patties and she opened the square tin box with the red coals in a pan in the sealed-off lower shelf. His head swam a little when he saw the crisp-flaked pastry and smelt the seasoned meat-smelling scent come up to him. Oh Jesus, Jesus Christ, but I'm hungry. Oh God, but a man shouldn't be able to get so damn hungry. He paid her with Gerald Hayes' half-crown and grabbed the warming, greasy paper bag of patties. He had almost finished one while she was counting his change. He hardly noticed the fire of red pepper and smoking hot meat on his tongue.

After he had eaten the patties, standing there in the street before the old woman, he went into a bar and the girl behind the counter gave him a big glass of iced water. He went out again into the white glare and the sticky, wet-sugar smell of the street. He scraped a match and lit a cigarette; the half-cigarette he had saved since morning. He drew it in his lungs a long while before he breathed it out slowly; feeling the tobacco blunt his sharp nerves.

He went down the street slowly, wondering what to do with the afternoon; thinking how good it would be if he got a job and Lyn wouldn't have to work when her time came near. When he saw Ladybird coming along the street, on the opposite sidewalk, he tried to look away; hoped that Ladybird wouldn't see him: heard, reluctantly, Ladybird's flat, arrogant voice calling to him across the street. He went over.

Ladybird was five foot three and thick as a saucepan. His body was drum-hard with sheets of magnificent muscle. His face was ugly and intelligent, with dead-cold, small eyes. He said "'Lo, Reuben, I been askin' for you dis mawning down on de wharves. You want to have a drink wid me?" He put his hands in the pocket of his sharp-creased, blue, tropical trousers and jingled what sounded like five pounds of silver.

When they were having the third rum and water in the same bar Reuben had gone into after eating his patties, Ladybird asked Reuben if he was working.

"No," said Reuben. "I ain't workin' yet."

"Too bad," said Ladybird. "You want to work for me?"

"No," Reuben told him. "You know dat, Ladybird. I don't want to work in your racket. What happen when dem catch me peddlin' dem ganja cigarettes? You tell me dat, eh?"

Ladybird said softly, "I ain't forcin' you to work for me. Indeed, I don' know why I bodder wid a damn stupid white-people's fool like you, except you is my brudder an' I don' like to see you all limp an' beat out." He laughed briefly, with a decisive, bitten-off gasp. "Have another drink," he said. It was an order. They had two more. Ladybird drinking them quickly, then waiting tensely and restlessly for Reuben to finish. Tapping his fingers, shifting on the balls of his feet, always looking around. "Come outside," he told Reuben. "I want to talk to you."

He flung some money on the counter and went out with a rolling swagger, not waiting for change. Reuben followed him slowly.

When they were in the street, Ladybird took Reuben's arm. He held it hard and Reuben could feel the constant electric intoxication of the man transfer to him, more powerfully than the rum. Ladybird began to talk in a hard, unavoidable whisper.

"Look, Reuben, me brudder, I don' like to see you like dis, you know. You is me family. If you won' work for me, an you can't get work oderwise, why you don' listen to me? Listen to me, bwoy! Lis'en good! You wan' to earn some money, easy?"

"Lawd God, yes," Reuben told him. "Hard or easy, I want de money. I want it bad."

"Den lis'en, you damn fool, lis'en good. You ever go out by de Palisadoes?"

"One Sunday," Reuben said, "One Sunday I go out dere to swim."

"Alright," said Ladybird, "den lis'en." They had been walking down the sidewalk, but now he stopped and faced Reuben. He talked rapidly and clearly; in a low voice, but not wasting a word. When he had finished Reuben said: "I couldn't do dat, Ladybird. I couldn't do dat, Ladybird. No sir, I couldn't do dat."

"Oh Jesus God," said Ladybird. "You is coward. You is coward like a dawg. You is coward like a bitch dawg wid pup in her belly. What happen to you? You wan' to live like a beggar all your life?"

"No," said Reuben. "I don' wan' dat."

"Den why you don' try what I tell you? Lawd God, it is so dam soft."

"I is afraid," said Reuben. "I is afraid of what happen to Lyn if dem catch me an' lock me up."

"Alright," Ladybird barked impatiently, "an' I tell you dem don' catch you. Jesus Christ, bwoy, all you do is go out dere 'bout t'ree o'clock an hide in de bush. 'Bout five, de brown men dem come out wid de women. A little lovin', an' den dem go in for a swim. Dat's when you go for de man's trouser pocket an' de woman's handbag. Don' bodder wid de rest, except de cigarette case and de vanity case is good stuff. Lawd judge me, it is easy. You know who I give dat job to? Little piss-arse ganja boys. It's all dey are good for. It's as easy as dat. Of course, it take plannin'. Not too often in de same spot. An' Jesus Christ, I have to watch out for dem goddam amateurs. Dey could ruin de business if I didn't put my boys on dem. If you want it, I'll lay it open for you dis afternoon. An' tomorrow too, if you don' have it lucky today."

"It ain't I is coward," said Reuben. "It is only I is so fraid 'bout Lyn. De baby soon comin' an' everyt'ing. Oh God, Ladybird, if I in prison she don' eat, you know."

"Alright, alright," said Ladybird, his brother, pushing his square, ugly face close to Reuben's. "Dem won' catch you. But if dey do, I will look after Lyn an' de pickney till you come out. I don't mind givin' money to a woman, but I don' like givin' you. It don' do you no good; it don' do you no good at all."

Reuben remembered the ten pounds or so he had gotten out of Ladybird in small loans. He winced a little inside him. Also, very suddenly, he felt the dead weight of night; all at once it was right there in his stomach; tasting bitter on his tongue.

Night on the steps with the other men who hadn't got work. Tonight, and all the other dead nights; waiting on the steps for the women to come down from the houses under the foothills where they worked during the day as servants.

"Mebbe," he said, "mebbe it is not such a bad idea, Ladybird." Something more than the rum he had taken warmed him pleasantly, gave him confidence. "Jesus," he said, "it sound so damn easy."

Ladybird grinned. "Easy," he said. "It's easy as ever. I'll get word to the boys you're working for me now. Don't go out till about t'ree or half past. You know de old wreck, de old Haitian ship dat lies out dere on de Palisadoes? Yes? I don' send anyone dere for a long time now. Dat's your spot today. An' tomorrow if you don' have luck today. I'm givin' you dat spot, Reuben; de whole Palisadoes is my territory." He jingled a fanfare of the silver in his pocket. "Also," said Ladybird, "I have to give you a bunch of keys. Sometimes de people dem lock de car-door. Dese are special keys. Dey will open any door, so don't lose dem. Dey are very valuable."

AFTERNOON

He lay flat along the warm sand, among the seagrapes, squinting through the green at the man and the woman making love. They were doing it about ten yards from where he was.

He felt an easy, happy confidence and a completely sympathetic enjoyment in the man's grunting pleasure and the woman's passive abandon. They were both of them very fair brown people of the sort who probably worked in the front office of a downtown bank. The man was tall and looked very powerful, with gaunt heavy bones. The woman was slim and delicately fine; her hair was so good she might have been white. They had come driving up about half past four, in a big grey Oxford; just when Reuben had been listening to the surf booming on the other side of the dunes for an hour.

They had parked in the sand about fifteen yards away; and they had undressed in the car. Then they had walked down in their bathing suits, deeper among the tangle of sea grapes, out of sight from the road, to make love, and then to swim in the pleasant warmth at the end of a sticky day; with the sunlight laid across the water in hard bright bands and the sour-sweet, salty smell of mangroves and shore-water heavy in the air.

Now they were having a wonderful time and looked so good and happy that Reuben hoped he would not burst out laughing with love and the feeling of comradeship that fired his blood.

They picked up their bathing suits and put them on; then they went out of the shelter of the foliage; their limbs moved with the lazy, slow freedom of complete safety, and they entered the bright sun and calm water near the shore.

Reuben watched them swim about twenty yards out and begin to tread water; they were talking and laughing in relaxed soft voices. Reuben began to crawl without a sound towards the car; he crawled, dragging his belly over the warm sand, through the bushes, so he would come out on the far side of the car.

As Ladybird had told him might happen, the door was locked. He took the big bunch of keys Ladybird had given him out of his pocket; he began to try them in the lock on the handle. He had found the one that fitted and was opening the door when the big man came round the back of the car. He was dripping from the sea and he must have come very silently, but the sand was spurting away under his feet with the force of his heavy-swinging, determined rush.

"You goddam black bitch," he said, and hit Reuben in the mouth.

In the vague, grey-black distance Reuben heard the woman scream. But it was not important. He was rolling on the sand, sick and dizzy, his mouth hurting: trying to get up. He was badly frightened; full of a cold fright that clogged his limbs. Then he felt the man's hand in his collar, and the sand scraped away suddenly as he was jerked upright, and then the big heavy fist suddenly crunched into his face and he felt his head going back and back and his neck suddenly full of agony and the sting of sand on his shoulders as the ground flung the breath out of his body.

Through a mist of dancing red and yellow and bright silver specks he saw the man's furious, brutal face bend over him, and as he rolled away desperately his fingers, scrabbling in the dry sand, struck the neck of the old half-buried beer bottle, a relict of some old picnic. Even after the big man had fallen in a stiff twitching heap, Reuben went on hitting him with the stub of the shattered bottle. He hit at him blindly, in a ferocious terror, hardly seeing the face dissolve in meaty ruin beneath the jagged glass. By the car the woman screamed and screamed, like an animal in a spring trap. He looked up after a little and said in an irritable and bewildered voice, "Why you don' hush you damn mout'?"

When he got to his feet, she turned to run. She ran towards the sea and Reuben followed her. She was still screaming when he caught her. She continued to scream, and to struggle, in a hopeless, very tired way, when he told her to stop. He put his fingers over her mouth to stifle her wild volume of despair. She bit his fingers but he did not feel it; only saw his blood flow with a blank curiosity. He did not know for quite a while that he had strangled her; but his fingers were stiff when she slipped from his hands to the beach.

All around him, then, it was enormously still. Still as death under the huge pale sky. The man's blood had spattered his shirt and trousers. Across the harbour the white city in the late afternoon sun looked near but yet remote, like a still flashed onto a deep screen.

He did not get back to his room till very late. He came in across the yard, keeping close to the shadow of the fence so the people would not see the blood on his clothes.

He had waited out on the Palisadoes until dark, before walking back to town; sitting on the dunes, about half a mile from where he had killed them, facing the open sea. Out there the sweat of agony and fear had covered his cold skin and his mouth had grown dry and nasty when he thought of what he had done. Sitting there, huddled over the tight discomfort of his stomach, he had wondered if he would ever be able to eat again. His breath came out like sobbing, and the world reeled and fell in on him.

Now, as he ran up the steps leading to the room, he wondered if anyone had found the bodies yet. He was very tired, and a huge tiredness had turned his legs to tubes full of water.

Lyn was lying on the bed when he came in: the light was turned down very low, and she looked soft, lost and helpless when he bent over her.

She said: "Where you been? You is late. You get a job?" "No," he said.

"You mus' be hungry," she said "Missis give me a bit of chicken fe' bring home tonight."

"I is not hungry," he told her. He felt the contraction of his stomach at the thought of food.

She sat up in bed instantly.

"Now don' talk foolishness," she said. "Big man like you, walk all day an' you tell me you not hungry. Sit down now an' I will bring it to you. I eat already up at de house."

Reuben pulled out a chair and sat down at the table. He felt stiffness seize him, and he could have screamed aloud at the dead heavy fear in him. Lyn turned up the lamp; she came over to the table with the brown paper bag which held the chicken which she had taken from the little attaché-case lying on the floor beside the bed.

When she saw him close she said: "What happen to your face?"

Reuben felt his lip and his cheekbone, where the big man's fists had marked and swollen him.

"I did have a fight today," he told her. "A man trouble me an' I did beat him up."

She suddenly put down the chicken; feeling the chill of his toneless voice run up her spine. She looked at him closer.

"Lawd God, Reuben," she said. "What happen?" She saw the blood on his clothes and leaned over the table. He could see by the movements of her cheeks that she was trying not to vomit.

"What happen?" she said.

"I tell you, I had a fight."

"What happen?"

So he told her: watching the skin of her face turn rough and grey.

When he had finished she said in a small, drowning voice: "What we gwine do, Reuben? Jesus, Reuben, what we gwine do?

"I don' know," he said. "Mebbe dem don' find out, eh? Nobody see me, you know. If dem don' see me dem can't find out. I didn't take nuttin'. Not a t'ing. Dem can't prove it was me."

They both wondered, then, if it was always going to be as bad as this before they came for him.

At the Stelling

"Dis one is no boss fe' we, Dunnie," Son-Son say. "I don' like how him stay. Dis one is boss fe' messenger an' women in department office, but not fe' we."

"Shut your mout'," I tell him. "Since when a stupid black nigger can like and don't like a boss in New Holland? What you goin' do? Retire an' live 'pon your estate?" But I know say that Son-Son is right.

The two of we talk so at the back of the line; Son-Son carrying the chain, me with the level on the tripod. The grass stay high and the ground hard with sun. It is three mile to where the Catacuma run black past the stelling, and even the long light down the sky can't strike a shine from Catacuma water. You can smell Rooi Swamp, dark and sweet and wicked like a woman in a bad house back in Zuyder Town. Nothing live in Rooi Swamp except snake; nothing live in a bad woman. In all South America there is no swamp like the Rooi; not even in Brazil; not even in Cayenne. The new boss, Mister Cockburn, walk far ahead with the little assistant man, Mister Bailey. Nobody count the assistant. Him only come down to the Catacuma to learn. John stay close behind them, near to the rifle. The other rest of the gang file out upon the trail between them three and me and Son-Son. Mister Cockburn is brand-new from head to foot. New hat, new bush-shirt, new denim pant, new boot. Him walk new.

"Mister Cockburn!" John call, quick and sharp. "Look!"

I follow the point of John's finger and see the deer. It fat and promise tender and it turn on the hoof-tip like deer always do, with the four tip standing on a nickel and leaving enough bare to make a cent change, before the spring into high grass. Mister Cockburn unship the rifle, and *pow* – if was all cow, then him shoot plenty grass for us to eat.

"Why him don't give John de rifle?" Son-Son say.

"Because the rifle is Government," I tell him, "and Mister Cockburn is Government. So it is him have a right to de rifle."

Mister Cockburn turn and walk back. He is a tall, high-mulatto man, young and full in body, with eyes not blue and not green, but coloured like the glass of a beer bottle. The big hat make him look like a soldier in the moving pictures.

"Blast this sun," he say, loud, to John. "I can't see a damn thing in the glare; it's right in my eyes." The sun is falling down the sky behind us, but maybe him think we can't see that too.

John don't answer but only nod once, and Mister Cockburn turn and walk on, and I know say that if I could see John's face it would be all Carib buck. Sometimes you can see where the Indian lap with it, but other times it is all Indian and closed like a prison gate; and I knew say, too, that it was this face Mister Cockburn did just see.

"Trouble dere, soon," Son-Son say, and him chin point to John and then to Mister Cockburn. "Why Mister Hamilton did have to get sick, eh, Dunnie? Dat was a boss to have."

"Whatever trouble to happen is John's trouble," I tell him. "John's trouble and Mister Cockburn's. Leave it. You is a poor naygur wid no schooling, five pickney and a sick woman. Dat is trouble enough for you."

But in my heart I find agreement for what stupid Son-Son have to say. If I have only known what trouble –

No. Life don't come so. It only come one day at a time. Like it had come every day since we lose Mister Hamilton and Mister Cockburn take we up to survey the Catacuma drainage area in Mister Hamilton's stead.

The first day we go on the savannah beyond the stelling, I know say that Mister Cockburn is frighten. Frighten, and hiding his frighten from himself. The worst kind of frighten. You hear frighten in him voice when he shout at we to keep the chain straight and plant the markers where him tell us. You see frighten when him try to work us, and himself, one hour after midday, when even the alligators hide in the water. And you understand frighten when him try to run the camp at the stelling as if we was soldier and him was a general. But all that is because he is new and it would pass but for John. Because of John everything remain bad. From the first day when John try to treat him as he treat Mister Hamilton.

You see, John and Mister Hamilton was like one thing, except that Mister Hamilton have schooling and come from a big family in Zuyder Town. But they each suck from a Carib woman and from the first both their spirit take. When we have Mister Hamilton as boss, whatever John say we do, as if it was Mister Hamilton say it, and at night when Mister Hamilton lie off in the big Berbice chair on the verandah and him and John talk it sound like one mind and two tongue. That's how it sound to the rest of we when we sit down the steps and listen to them talk. Only when Mister Cockburn come back up the river with we, after Mister Hamilton take sick, we know say all that is change. For Mister Cockburn is frighten and must cut down John's pride, and from that day John don't touch the rifle and don't come to the verandah except to take orders and for Mister Cockburn to show that gang foreman is only gang foreman and that boss is always boss.

Son-Son say true, I think. Trouble is to come between John and Mister Cockburn. Poor John. Here in the bush, him is a king, but in New Zuyder him is just another poor half-buck without a job and Mister Cockburn is boss, and some he cast down and some he raiseth up.

Ahead of we, I see Mister Cockburn trying to step easy and smooth, as if we didn't just spend seven hours on the savannah. Him is trying hard but very often the new boot kick black dirt from the trail. That is all right, I think. Him will learn. Him don't know say that even John hold respect for the sun on the Catacuma. The sun down here on the savannah is like the centurion in the Bible who say to one man, Come, and he cometh, and to another, Go, and he goeth. Like it say Go to Mister Hamilton. For it was a man sick bad we take down to the mouth of the river that day after he fall down on the wharf at the stelling. And it was a nearly dead man we drive up the coast road one hundred mile to Zuyder Town. Afterward the government doctor tell Survey that he must stay in the office forevermore and even Mister Hamilton, who think him love the bush and the swamp and the forest more than life itself, was grateful to the doctor for those words.

So it was it did happen with Mister Hamilton, and so it was Mister Cockburn come to we.

Three weeks we is on the Catacuma with Mister Cockburn, and every new day things stay worse than the last.

In the morning, when him come out with the rifle, him shout: "Dunnie! Take the corial across the river and put up these bottles." And he fling the empty rum and beer bottle down the slope to me and I get into the corial and paddle across the river, and put the necks over seven sticks on the other bank. Then him and the little assistant, Mister Bailey, stay on the verandah and fire across the river, each spelling each, until the bottle is all broken.

And John, down by the river, in the soft morning light, standing in the corial we have half buried in the water, half drawn upon the bank, washing himself all over careful like an Indian and not looking to the verandah.

"John!" Mister Cockburn shout, and laugh bad. "Careful, eh, man. Mind a perai don't cut off your balls."

We have to stand in the corial because perai is bad on the Catacuma and will take off your heel and your toe if you stand in the river six inches from the bank. We always joke each other about it, but not the way Mister Cockburn joke John. That man know what he is doing and it is not nice to hear.

John say nothing. Him stand in the still-water catch of the corial we half sink and him wash him whole body like an Indian and wash him mouth out and listen to Mister Cockburn fire at the bottle across the river. Only we know how John need to hold that rifle. When it come to rifle and gun him is all Indian, no African in it at all. Rifle to him is like woman to we. Him don't really hold a rifle, him make love with it. And I think how things go in Mister Hamilton's time when him and John stand on the verandah in the morning and take seven shots, break seven bottle, and out in the bush they feel shame if four shot fire and only three piece of game come back. Mister Hamilton is a man think hard all the time. And the question he ask! "Dunnie," he ask, "what do you see in your looking-glass?" or, "Do you know, Dunnie, that this country has had its images broken on the wheels of false assumptions? Arrogance and servility. Twin criminals pleading for the mercy of an early death." That is how Mister Hamilton talk late at night when him lie off in the big Berbice chair and share him mind with we.

After three weeks on the Catacuma, Mister Cockburn and most of we go down the river. Mister Cockburn to take him plans to the department, and the rest of we because nothing to do when him is gone. All the way down the river John don't say a word. Him sit in the boat bows and stare down the black water as if it is a book giving him a secret to remember. Mister Cockburn is loud and happy, for him feel, we know say, now, who is boss, and him begin to lose him frighten spirit.

"Remember, now," him say in the Department yard at Zuyder Town. "Eight o'clock sharp on Tuesday morning. If one of you is five minutes late, the truck leaves without you. Plenty of men between here and the Catacuma glad to get work." We laugh and say, "Sure, boss, sure," because we know say that already him is not so new as him was and that him is only joking. Only John don't laugh but walk out of the yard and down the street.

Monday night, John come to my house; I is living in a little place between the coolie cinema and the dockyard.

"Dunnie," he say, "Dunnie, you have fifteen dollar?"

"Jesus," I say, "what you need fifteen dollar for, man? Dat is plenty, you know?"

"All right," he say. "You don't have it. I only ask."

Him turn, as if it was the time him ask and I don't have no watch.

"Hold on, hold on," I tell him. "I never say I don't have fifteen dollar. I just say, what you want it for?"

"Lend me. I don't have enough for what I want. As we pay off next month, you get it back. My word to God."

I go into the house.

"Where de money?" I ask the woman.

"What you want it for?" she ask. "You promise say we don't spend dat money until we marry and buy furnitures. What you want tek it now for?"

"Just tell me where it stay," I tell her. "Just tell me. Don't mek me have to find it, eh?"

"Thank you, Dunnie," John say when I bring him the fifteen dollar. "One day you will want something bad. Come to me then."

And him gone up the street so quick you scarcely see him pass under the light.

The next morning, in the truck going down to the boat at the Catacuma mouth, we see what John did want fifteen dollar for.

"You have a licence for that?" Mister Cockburn ask him, hard and quick, when he see it.

"Yes," John say and stow the new Ivor-Johnson repeater with his gear up in the boat bows.

"All right," Mister Cockburn say. "I hope you do. I don't want any un-licensed guns on my camp."

Him and John was never born to get on.

We reach the stelling late afternoon. The bungalow stand on the bluff above the big tent where we sleep, and Zacchy, who we did leave to look to the camp, wait on the wharf waving to us.

When we passing the gear from the boat, John grab his bundle by the string and swing it up. The string break and shirt, pant and handkerchief fly out to float on the water. Them float but the new carton of .32 ammunition fall out too and we see it for a second, green in the black water as it slide to the bottom and the mud and the perai. Mister Bailey, the little assistant, look sorry, John look sick, and Mister Cockburn laugh a little up in the back of him nose. "Is that all you had?" him ask.

"Yes," John say. "I don't need no more than that for three weeks."

"Too bad," Mister Cockburn reply. "Too bad. Rotten luck. I might be able to spare you a few from stores."

Funny how a man who can stay decent with everybody always find one other who turn him bad.

Is another three weeks we stay up on the survey. We triangulate all the stretch between the Rooi Swamp and the first forest. Things is better this time. Mister Cockburn don't feel so rampageous to show what a hard boss him is. Everything is better except him and John. Whenever him and John speak, one voice is sharp and empty and the other voice is dead, and empty too. Every day him give John two, three cartridge, and John go out and come back with two, three piece of game. A deer and a labba, maybe. Or a bush pig and an agouti. Whatever ammunition John get, him bring back meat to match. And, you know, I think that rowel Mister Cockburn's spirit worse than anything else John do. Mister Cockburn is shooting good, too, and we is eating plenty meat, but him don't walk with the gun like John. Who could ever? Not even Mister Hamilton.

The last Saturday before we leave, John come to Mister Cockburn. It is afternoon and work done till Monday. Son-Son and me is getting the gears ready for a little cricket on the flat piece under the kookorit palms. The cricket gears keep in the big room with the other rest of stores and we hear every word John and Mister Cockburn say.

"No, John," Mister Cockburn tell him. "We don't need any meat. We're leaving Tuesday morning. We have more than enough now." Him voice sleepy and deep from the Berbice chair.

"Sell me a few rounds, Mister Cockburn," John say. "I will give you store price for a few rounds of .32."

"They're not mine to sell," Mister Cockburn say, and him is liking the whole business so damn much his voice don't even hold malice as it always do for John. "You know every round of ammunition here belongs to Survey. I have to indent and account for every shot fired."

Him know, like we know, that Survey don't give a lime how much shot fire up in the bush so long as the men stay happy and get meat.

"You can't give three shot, Mister Cockburn?" John say. You know how bad John want to use the new repeater when you hear him beg.

"Sorry, John," Mister Cockburn say. "Have you checked the caulking on the boat? I don't want us shipping any water when we're going down on Tuesday."

A little later all of we except John go out to play cricket. Mister Cockburn and Mister Bailey come too, and each take captain of a side. We play till the parrots come talking across the river to the kookorits and the sky turn to green and fire out on the savannah. When we come back to the camp John is gone. Him take the corial and gone.

"That damn buck," Mister Cockburn say to Mister Bailey. "Gone up the river to his cousins, I suppose. We won't see him until Monday morning now. You can take an Indian out of the bush, but God Almighty Himself can't take the bush out of the Indian."

Monday morning, we get up and John is there. Him is seated on the stelling and all you can see of him face is the teeth as him grin and the cheeks swell up shiny with pleasure. Lay out on the stelling before him is seven piece of game. Three deer, a labba and three bush pig. None of we ever see

John look so. Him tired till him thin and grey, but happy and proud till him can't speak.

"Seven," him say at last and hold up him finger. "Seven shots, Dunnie. That's all I take. One day and seven shot."

Who can stay like an Indian with him game and no shot gone wide?

"What's this?" a voice call from up the verandah and we look and see Mister Cockburn in the soft, white-man pyjamas lean over to look at we on the stelling. "Is that you, John? Where the devil have you been?"

"I make a little trip, Mister Cockburn," John say. Him is so proud and feel so damn sweet him like even Mister Cockburn. "I make a little trip. I bring back something for you to take back to town. Come and make your choice, sir."

Mister Cockburn is off the verandah before the eye can blink, and we hear the fine red slipper go slap-slap on the patch down the bluff. Him come to the wharf and stop short when him see the game. Then him look at John for a long time and turn away slow and make water over the stelling edge and come back, slow and steady.

"All right," him say, and him voice soft and feel bad in your ears, like you did stumble in the dark and put your hand into something you would walk round. "All right, John. Where did you get the ammunition? Who gave it to you, eh?" Him voice go up and break like a boy's voice when the first hairs begin to grow low down on him belly.

"Mister Cockburn," John say, so crazy proud that even now him want to like the man and share pride with him. "I did take the rounds, sir. From your room. Seven shot I take, Mister Cockburn, and look what I bring you back. Take that deer, sir, for yourself and your family. Town people never taste meat like that."

"You son of a bitch," Mister Cockburn reply. "You damned impertinent, thieving son of a bitch. Bailey!" – and him voice scream until Mister Bailey come out to the verandah. "Bailey! Listen to this. We have a thief in the camp. This beauty here feels that the Government owes him his ammunition."

"What else did you take?" Him voice sound as if a rope tie round him throat.

"What else I take?" John look as if him try to kiss a woman and she slap him face. "How I could take anything, Mister Cockburn? As if I am a thief. Seven little shot I take from the carton. You don't even remember how many rounds you did have left. How many you did have leave, eh? Tell me that."

"Don't back-chat me, you bloody thief!" Mister Cockburn yell. "This is your last job with the Survey, you hear me? I'm going to fire your arse as soon as we get to the river mouth. And don't think this game is yours to give away. You shot it with government ammunition. With *stolen* government ammunition. Here! Dunnie! Son-Son! Zacchy! Get that stuff up to the house. Zacchy, gut them and hang 'em. I'll decide what to do with them later."

John stay as still as if him was dead. Only when we gather up the game and a kid deer drop one splash of dark stomach blood onto the boards him draw one long breath and shiver.

"Now," Mister Cockburn say, "get the hell out of here! Up to the tent. You don't work for me anymore. I'll take you down the river on Tuesday and that's all. And if I find one dollar missing from my wallet I'm going to see you behind bars."

It is that day I know say how nothing so bad before but corruption and rottenness come worse after. None of we could forget John's face when we pick up him game. For we Negro, and for the white man and for the mulatto man, game is to eat sometimes, or it is to play to shoot. But for the Indian, oh God, game that him kill true is life everlasting. It is manhood.

When we come back early in the afternoon, with work done, we don't see John. But the corial still there, and the engine boat, and we know that him not far. Little later, when Zacchy cook, I fill a billy pot and go out to the kookorits. I find him there in the grass.

"John," I say. "Don't tek it so. Mister Cockburn young and foolish and don't mean harm. Eat, John. By the time we reach river mouth tomorrow everyt'ing will be well again. Do, John. Eat dis."

John look at me and it is one black Indian Carib face stare like statue into mine. All of him still, except the hands that hold the new rifle and polish, polish, polish with a rag until the barrel shine blue like a Chinee whore hair.

I came back to the stelling. Mister Cockburn and Mister Bailey lie in two deck chair under the tarpaulin, enjoying the afternoon breeze off the river. Work done and they hold celebration with a bottle. The rest of the gang sit on the boards and drink too. Nothing sweeter than rum and river water.

"Mister Cockburn," I tell him, "I don't like how John stay. Him is hit hard, sah."

"Oh, sit down, Dunnie," him say. "Have a drink. That damned buck needs a lesson. I'll take him back when we reach Zuyder Town. It won't do him any harm to miss two days' pay."

So I sit, although I know say I shouldn't. I sit and I have one drink, and then two, and then one more. And the Catacuma run soft music round the piles of the stelling. All anybody can feel is that work done and we have one week in Zuyder Town before money need call we to the bush again.

Then as I go to the stelling edge to dip water in the mug I look up and see John. He is coming down from the house, gliding on the path like Jesus across the Sea of Galilee, and I say, "Oh God, Mister Cockburn! Where you leave the ammunition, eh?"

But it is already too late to say that.

The first shot catch Mister Cockburn in the forehead and him drop back into the deck chair, peaceful and easy, like a man call gently from sleep who only half wake. And I shout, "Dive-oh, Mister Bailey!" and as I drop from the stelling into the black Catacuma water, I feel something like a marabunta wasp sting between my legs and know say I must be the first thing John ever shoot to kill that him only wound.

I sink far down in that river and already, before it happen, I can feel perai chew at my fly button and tear off my cod, or alligator grab my leg to drag me to drowning. But God is good. When I come up the sun is still there and I strike out for the little island in the river opposite the stelling. The river is full of death that pass you by, but the stelling holds a walking death like the destruction of Apocalypse.

I make ground at the island and draw myself into the mud and the bush and blood draw after me from between my legs. And when I look back at the stelling, I see Mister Cockburn lie down in him deck chair, as if fast asleep, and Mister Bailey lying on him face upon the boards, with him hands under him stomach, and Zacchy on him back with him arms flung wide like a baby, and three more of the gang, Will, Benjie and Sim, all sprawl off on the boards, too, and a man more, the one we call Venezuela, fallen into the grass, and a last one, Christopher, walking like a chicken without a head until him drop close to Mister Bailey and cry out once before death hold him. The other seven gone. Them vanish. All except Son-Son, poor foolish Son-Son, who make across the flat where we play cricket, under the kookorits and straight to Rooi Swamp.

"Oh Jesus, John!" him bawl as him run. "Don't kill me, John! Don't kill me, John!"

And John standing on the path, with the repeater still as the finger of God in him hands, aim once at Son-Son, and I know say how, even at that distance, him could break Son-Son's back clean in the middle. But him lower the gun, and shrug and watch Son-Son into the long grass of the savannah and into the swamp. Then him come down the path and look at the eight dead men.

"Dunnie!" him call. "I know you is over there. How you stay?"

I dig a grave for the living into the mud.

"Dunnie!" him call again. "You hurt bad? Answer me, man. I see you, you know? Look!"

A bullet bury itself one inch from my face and mud smack into my eye.

"Don't shoot me, John," I beg. "I lend you fifteen dollar, remember?"

"I finish shooting, Dunnie," him say. "You hurt bad?"

"No," I tell him the lie. "I all right."

"Good," him say from the stelling. "I will bring the corial come fetch you."

"No, John!" I plead with him. "Stay where you is. Stay there! You don't want kill me now." But I know say how demon guide a Carib hand sometimes and make that hand cut throats. "Stay there, John!"

Him shrug again and squat beside Mister Cockburn's chair, and lift the fallen head and look at it and let the head fall again. And I wait. I wait and bleed and suffer, and think how plenty women will cry and plenty children bawl for them daddy when John's work is known in Zuyder Town. I think all these things and watch John the way I would watch a bushmaster snake and bleed in suffering until dark fall. All night I lie there until God take pity and close my eye and mind.

When my mind come back to me, it is a full day. John gone from the stelling and I can see him sit on the steps up at the house watching the river. The dead stay same place where he drop them. Fever burn in me, but the leg stop bleed and I dip water from the river and drink.

The day turn above my head until I hear a boat engine on the far side of the bend, and in a little bit a police launch come up midstream and make for the stelling. When they draw near, one man step to the bows with a boat-hook, and then the rifle talk from the steps and the man yell, hold him wrist and drop to the deck. Him twist and wriggle behind the cabin quicker than a lizard. I hear an Englishman's voice yell in the cabin and the man at the wheel find reverse before the yell come back from the savannah. The boat go downstream a little, then nose into the overhang of the bank, where John's rifle can't find them. I call out once and they come across to the island and take me off on the other side, away from the house. And is when I come on board that I see how police know so quick about what happen. For Son-Son, poor foolish old Son-Son, who I think still hide out in the swamp, is there. Him have on clothes not his own, and him is scratched and torn as if him had to try to wrestle a jaguar.

As then I learn that Son-Son did run straight as a peccary pig, all night, twenty mile across Rooi Swamp where never any man had even put him foot before. Him did run until him drop down in the camp of a coolie rancher bringing cattle down to the coast, and they did take him from there down to the nearest police post. When him tell police the story, they put him in the jeep and drive like hell for the river mouth and the main station.

"Lord witness, Son-Son," I say, "you was born to hang. How you didn't meet death in Rooi Swamp, eh?"

Him just look frighten and tremble, and the sergeant laugh.

"Him didn't want to come upriver with we," he say. "Superintendent nearly have to tie him before him would step on the boat."

"Sergeant," the superintendent say. Him was the Englishman I hear call out when John wound the policeman. "Sergeant, you take three men and move in on him from behind the house. Spread out well. I'll take the front approach with the rest. Keep low, you understand. Take your time."

"Don't do it, Super," I beg him. "Look how John stay in that house up there. River behind him and a clear view before. Him will see you as you move one step. Don't do it."

Him look at me angry with the white eyebrow draw together in him red face.

"Do you think I'm going to leave him up there?" he say. "He's killed eight and already tried to kill one of my men."

Him is bad angry for the constable who sit on the bunk and holding him wrist in the red bandage.

"No, Super," I tell him. "John don't *try* to kill you. If him did try then you would have take one dead man out of the river. Him only want to show you that him can sting."

But what use a poor black man talk to police. The sergeant and him three stand on the cabin roof, hold onto the bank and drag themself over. Then the Super with him five do the same. I can hear them through the grass like snakes on them stomach. John let them come a little way to the house, and then, with him first shot, him knock the Super's black cap off, and with him second, him plug the sergeant in the shoulder. The police rifles talk back for a while, and Son-Son look at me. When the police come back, I take care to say no word. The sergeant curse when the Super pour Dettol on the wound and beg the Super to let him go back and bring John down.

"We'll get him," the Super say. "He knows it. He knows he doesn't stand a chance."

But him voice can't reach John to tell him that, and when them try again one man come back with him big toe flat and bloody in the police boot. When I go out, though, and walk along the bank to the stelling and lay out the bodies decent and cover them with canvas from the launch, it could have been an empty house up there on the bluff.

Another hour pass and the police begin to fret, and I know say that them is going to try once more. I want to tell them don't go, but them is police and police don't like hear other men talk. And is then, as we wait, that we hear a next engine, an outboard, and round the bend come a Survey boat, and long before it draw up beside the overhang, my eye know Mister Hamilton as him sit straight and calm in the bows.

"Dunnie, you old fool," him say and hold me by the shoulders. "Why didn't you stop it? D'you mean to say you couldn't see it coming?"

Him smile to show me that the words is to hide sorrow. Him is the same Mister Hamilton. Dress off in the white shirt and white stocking him always wear, with the big linen handkerchief spread upon him head under the hat and hanging down the neck back to guard him from sun.

"I came as soon as I could," him say to the Super. "As soon as the police in Zuyder rang Survey and told us what you had 'phoned through."

You can see the Super is glad to have one of him own sort to talk with. More glad, though, because it is Mister Hamilton and Mister Hamilton's spirit make all trouble seem less.

"We might have to bomb him out," Super say. "I've never seen a man to shoot like that. He must be a devil. Do you think he's sane, Mister Hamilton?"

Mister Hamilton give a little smile that is not a smile. "He's sane now," he say. "If he wasn't he'd have blown your head off."

"What's he going to do?" Super ask.

Mister Hamilton lift him shoulder and shake him head. Then him go up to the cabin top and jump on the bank and walk to the stelling. Not a sign from the house.

I follow him and move the canvas from all the staring dead faces and him look and look and pass him hand, tired and slow, across him face.

"How did it go, Dunnie?" him ask. I tell him.

"You couldn't have stopped him?"

"No," I say. "Him did have pride to restore. Who could have stop that? You, maybe, Mister Hamilton. But I doubt me if even you."

"All right," him say. "All right."

Him turn and start to walk to the house.

"Come back, man," Super shout from where him lie in the grass on the bank. Mister Hamilton just walk on regular and gentle.

John's first bullet open a white wound in the boards by Mister Hamilton's left foot. The next one do the same by the right. Him never look or pause; even him back, as I watch, don't stiffen. The third shot strike earth before him and kick dirt onto him shoe.

"John!" him call, and Mister Hamilton have a voice like a howler monkey when him want. "John, if you make a ricochet and kill me, I'm going to come up there and break your ——ing neck."

Him walk on, easy and slow, up the path, up the steps, and into the house.

I sit by the dead and wait.

Little bit pass and Mister Hamilton come back. Him is alone, with a basket in him hand. Him face still. Like the face of a mountain lake, back in the interior, where you feel but can't see the current and the fullness of water below.

"Shirley," him call to the Super, "bring the launch up to the stelling. You'll be more comfortable here than where you are. It's quite safe. He won't shoot if you don't rush him."

I look into the basket him bring down from the house. It full of well-cooked labba. Enough there to feed five times the men that begin to gather on the stelling.

The Super look into the basket also, and I see a great bewilderment come into his face.

"Good God!" him say. "What's all this? What's he doing?" "Dunnie," Mister Hamilton say to me. "There's a bottle of rum in my boat. And some bread and a packet of butter. Bring them over for me, will you? Go on," him tell Super, "have some. John thought you might be getting hungry."

I go to the Survey boat and fetch out the rum and the bread and the butter. The butter wrap into grease paper and sink in a closed billy pot of water to keep it from the sun. I bring knife, also, and a plate and a mug for Mister Hamilton, and a billy full of river water for put into the rum. When everything come, him cut bread and butter it and pour rum for Super and himself, and take a leg of labba. When him chew the food, him eat like John. The jaws of him mouth move sideways and not a crumb drop to waste. The rest of we watch him and Super, and then we cut into the labba too, and pour liquor from the bottle. The tarpaulin stretch above we and the tall day is beginning to die over the western savannah.

"Why did he do it?" Super say and look at the eight dead lay out under the canvas. "I don't understand it, Hamilton. Christ! He *must* be mad."

Him lean over beside Mister Hamilton and cut another piece of labba from the basket.

"What does he think he can do?" him ask again. "If he doesn't come down I'm going to send down river for grenades. We'll have to get him out somehow."

Mister Hamilton sit and eat and say nothing. Him signal to me and I pass him the bottle. Not much left into it, for we all take a drink. Mister Hamilton tilt out the last drop and I take the billy and go to the stelling edge and draw a little water for Mister Hamilton and bring it back. Him draw the drink and put the mug beside him. Then him step from under the tarpaulin and fling the empty bottle high over Catacuma water. And as the bottle turn and flash against the dying sun, I see it fall apart in the middle and broken glass falling like raindrops as John's bullet strike.

We all watch and wait, for now the whole world stand still and wait with we. Only the water make soft music round the stelling.

Then from up the house there is the sound of one shot. It come to us sudden and short and distant, as if something close it round.

"All right," Mister Hamilton say to the Super. "You better go and bring him down now."

The Lost Country

Afterwards, when he was strong enough to walk, he used to go in the cool glow of first dusk to the river. Seated on a bollard, the boards of the narrow wharf still warm from the day's sun, he would let the huge sweep of brown water flow without hindrance through a mind which seemed to operate, when it did at all, in anguished, undirected spasms. One night he told himself that thought was trying to struggle free from confusion like a broken snake drowning in the swamp, and with the formation of that image he was suddenly well again. He could remember beyond the surging, white waters of the estuary and the dull scrub on the flat bank opposite, as far as Maraca, Overlook, the Narrows and the bleached rocks of Paramuni Rapids where the real forest began. He sat for a long time and restored the lost country slowly to his tattered mind, going up through the vaults and green-black shadows of the forest to the harsh, lemon light and dry-grass smell of the high savannas, where a line of men on the horizon seemed to walk not over the edge of the world but simply on and on into the secret reaches of the enormous sky.

When his wife called tentatively from the shadow of the warehouse at his back, he answered and heard his own voice for the first time in six months. During this time something not himself, something deeper even than the chaos, had spoken the forgotten simplicities of intercourse; but the words, once in space between him and another, had struck no echo.

"Yes?" he called; then strongly: "Yes, Daphne. I'm here. I was just coming."

He swung around on the bollard and watched her white dress become definite as she drew near in the light of the evening. As she came up beside him, he took her hand and kissed the fingers with tranquil and deliberate intimacy.

"I was worried," she said uncertainly. "It was getting so late. Aren't you hungry?"

He looked up at the handsome, solid-featured face in which a timid intuition of happiness had begun to stir cautiously. Then he smiled, and the desolate, careful discipline of the past half-year collapsed and she flung herself on to his lap, put her arm around his neck and cried easily against his shoulder.

"It's all right," he told her. "I'm all right now. It's all over."

"Oh, Harry," she said, "I thought it would never be over. I thought you'd never come back, Harry. Harry, darling."

"Poor girl," he said. "My poor old girl. Don't cry, honey. It's all over now. I was just sitting here, and I began to remember the interior. You know, everything about it, even the smell." He raised her chin and smiled again. "It's only fair, really. It nearly destroyed me, I guess, so it's only fair for it to give something back."

When he put his hand on the front of her dress and stroked it and the brown swell of her breast, she began to smile sensuously, with indulgent approval, and pressed against him until she realized that he was fondling her as a baby would explore a piece of velvet, with the absorbed innocence of pure learning.

But the next day, when he went to see the doctor to whom he owed his life and reason, he learned that it was not really over.

"You can't work in the bush again, Harry," his doctor told him. "If you try to go back, you'll be dead in two years."

"You're not serious," Harry Hamilton answered. "You don't mean that I have to spend the rest of my days on this stinking coast. That's a death sentence, Marie."

"Life sentence," Marie Rau said, and looked at him with wry, helpless compassion. "Listen, Harry. Listen good. What happened to you down on the Catacuma was simply the last of a lot of things. You're overexposed, Harry, don't you understand? Sometime in the last twenty years you walked too far and too fast one day. Maybe it was on a lot of days. Or maybe you got too much sun. Or too much fever. Or one bush ulcer too many. Take your pick. I think it was all of them together, and sunstroke on the Catacuma just meant that you had reached the end of something."

"I don't believe you," Harry Hamilton told her bleakly. "You've cooked this up with Daphne. It's an excuse to keep me from going inside again. She has wanted that for a long time."

"If it makes you feel any better," Marie Rau said, "you can believe that." She smiled at him and tossed her head in gentle mockery, and he grinned back without much amusement but with complete understanding.

"All right," he said. "Forgive and forget. I didn't mean what I said. I was just getting used to it."

"That's what I'm here for," she said, and rested her elbows on the desk, her long, beautiful hands clasped under her chin, and looked steadily at the big, wasted man before her.

She was an East Indian and had been the first woman of her race in the colony to defy the past by taking a profession. After she had come back, there had been a lonely, sterile time for her during which she had grown the remote, ironic dignity and sadness that had nothing to do with what she really was. Harry Hamilton had been her first patient, twenty years before, after she had been sitting for three months in an empty office beyond the always empty waiting-room. He had come to her to have his hand dressed where a badly held fishing line upriver had torn through to the bone. Hers was the first name-plate he had seen that morning as he walked up from the wharf, and he had come in because he was dizzy and nauseated with the pain of his swollen, infected flesh, but mainly because he had never been able to feel or think in the terms that an East Indian and a woman would be either less or more of a doctor than any other.

He was seventeen then to her twenty-five, in the first month of his articles as a surveyor, and beneath the fresh, Scottish colouring she had seen the profound, antique stamp of his Carib mother as, with stoical detachment, he watched her probe the reeking fissure across the palm of his hand. And sensing in the radiant, vulnerable candour of the boy's face something kindred, visionary and inarticulate, she had spoken out of the silent pride in which she had begun to harbour the nearly exhausted remnants of her own expectation and committed strength. Often, since then, she had wondered what would have happened to her in this colony of mediocre ambitions and insipid nostalgias if Harry Hamilton had not come into her life that morning.

Now she said: "What are you thinking, Harry?"

"I was trying to salvage something from the prospect," he answered, and shook his head slowly. "But there's nothing. We've destroyed the meaning of this country on the coast, Marie. You know that? First the Dutch. Then the English and the Africans. Masters and slaves both. They were united on that. Your people, too, although they came late. Only my mother's people know that you can't take the earth out of time, squeeze it into endless departments of use like – like the rooms in a house, but they don't have the words to tell us. I was beginning to understand, and maybe if I could have had another twenty years I would have found the words to convince you coast people. But not now. Not now."

When he was working again he still went to the river in the late afternoons before dark, to the same wharf and the same bollard, screened from the murmur of the town by the high, tarred wall of the warehouse. The ships came up the river, lifting as the long Atlantic took them over the bar, discharged their cargoes into the pungent caverns of wood near where he sat, and went back downstream, heavy with a return of copra, sugar, bauxite, hides and timber. Harry Hamilton watched them come and go with interest, without regret; he liked to see the stark light of the arc lamps transfiguring the decks, and the big cranes groping in the holds, and the efficient tumult of shining men. But with the coming of the wide, blunt-bowed river steamer around the bend from upstream, he would become suddenly alert. And when the jangling bell told him that it was about to begin the sluggish crab crawl across to its berth, he would rise and walk slowly down to the landing stage. Often there were men aboard whom he had known, and on those nights his wife learned not to expect him home until she saw him, very often at the breakfast table the next morning, his eyes alive and glittering, his face sallow with stale liquor, and his voice rough with too much talking.

Occasionally, too, he was able to join the department plane when it took the field officers and supplies up to the district stations. But in those places that he had known, looking out for a few hours over the country in which he had felt happy and meaningful, he understood the extent of his dispossession. He understood this and came back whenever he could, in the way that a man who has irrecoverably lost a woman will wait an hour on a street corner for her to pass with another, she now more remote, for ever untouchable, than if he had never known her, her smile at the other and her hand on his quite unreal actions, revealing the lost love with an appalling, magnified clarity, like an atom of coral sunk in pure, excluding glass. It was on one of these flights to the interior, at Shemarang on the Courenbice River, that he met Bargie.

They had flown up early in the morning as far as the cattle station at Haut Desir on the Venezuelan border, and early in the afternoon had come down the river to Shemarang. When you came in to land at Shemarang, a small Indian boy stood in the bow of a beached woodskin and threw stones into the water. The plane banked steeply above a high sandstone bluff on the far bank, and you saw a tilted, green-furred bed of forest and a faraway brown shining coil of river against a diagonal horizon; then, as abruptly as the next frame in a lantern-slide show, you were below the level of the tree-tops, with trees blurring into a wall of green-streaked brown and the river unravelling furiously like ribbon tugged from a spool. Then you saw the ripples spreading from the still surface of the landing basin as the little boy threw stones into the water, and the floats of the Norton struck just beyond the place where the farthest ripple was captured by the hard rush of the main stream. A leaping sheet of rust-tinged black water blotted the bank from view, and then, wavering and smeared at first, becoming clearer as the water ran from the glass, there appeared the moored corials and woodskins, the white sandy slope of the clearing, the tree stumps scattered on it like stubborn old teeth and, at the top of the slope, the three huts standing high on their great plugs of iron heart. The forest began close behind the huts, and even from the river you could see the tunnels going into the green and the deep shadows.

Now Harry Hamilton sat with Buster McKitterick, the pilot, in the largest of the huts, which was the general store, drinking beer and watching two Indians unload the supplies for the survey camp thirty miles up Shemarang Creek. The plane was lashed close to the shore, and a black man stood on one of the floats and directed the Indians as one of them handed the sacks of coffee, flour, sugar and tinned goods from the open cabin door to the other standing on the bank. It was cool and dark and restful in the general store, and the beer washed the engine fumes from the back of the throat.

"Have another?" Buster McKitterick asked.

"Yes," Harry Hamilton said. "Thanks."

The East Indian who owned the store came from behind the zinc-topped bar with two wet bottles and poured for them.

"Have a drink, Stephen," Buster McKitterick said.

"Well, thank you, Captain McKitterick," the East Indian said. "I will have a beer, sir."

He took the money from McKitterick and went back behind the bar and took another bottle from the big water-filled bucket and pried the cap off. He raised the bottle to McKitterick and Hamilton and drank. Then he leaned his elbows on the zinc and gazed through the open door at the men around the plane. He was young and very good-looking; handsome in the ripe, sculptured fashion of many East Indians. His hair looked as if it had been polished, and it was beginning to go grey at the sides and in the widow's peak.

"Niggers," the East Indian, Stephen, said reflectively, almost idly. "They don't wort' nuttin'. That nigger down there, Lloyd, him is the only one I know will do anyt'ing wid him life. An' dat's because him is a small-island man, from Barbados."

"What sort of talk is that, Stephen?" Harry Hamilton said in the same lazy and reflective voice. "How a damn' coolie like you can talk about niggers? If it wasn't for the pork knockers and timbermen buying your stores, how you would make a living?"

"And is hell I catch to get money out of dem sometimes," Stephen told him. "But is true what I say, Mister Hamilton. You must know is true. Niggers worse dan Indians, an' Gawd knows de bucks is bad enough. Lawd, de times I stay here an' see de pork knockers going down to Zuyder, each of dem wid a cartridge case holding, five, six, seven hundred pounds' worth of diamond. But you t'ink dey would put some of dat into anyt'ing? Not dem. Is fine clothes an' women an' spree until de money done, an' den back up de river to look for more diamond, What a people!"

"Stephen," Buster McKitterick said, "I do believe you're a racialist."

"What dat, Captain?" Stephen asked.

"He means that you believe in the master race, Stephen," Harry Hamilton told him. "Do you?"

"I don't know about master race," Stephen said seriously, "but I know say how Gawd give every people a sickness. De white man get greed, de Portugee get swell foot, we East Indian, weak chest, but de black man, him get de worst of all. Laziness."

"Now you see why we're a colony," Harry Hamilton said to McKitterick, who was an American. "The bloody British don't even have the trouble of divide and rule. We take care of the division for them." He looked at Stephen and shook his head with as much rueful amusement as despair.

"Go on, Stephen," McKitterick said. "There must be something good in our black brothers. Tell us something good."

"Yes," Stephen told them. "Dem is good for one t'ing. Spend money. Nobody can spend money like dem. An' nobody can beg like dem. Like de one I have living on me back dere now." He jerked his head over his shoulder at the shut door between the storeroom and the bar.

"Who is that?" Harry Hamilton said. "Anybody who can get something for nothing out of you, Stephen, must be worth knowing."

"Is an old pork knocker," Stephen said. "Damn' old madman called Bargie. Him was prospecting up beyond the falls and get sick. Him crawl in here one day like an old wild dog looking for a bush to die under. Well, I couldn't turn him away, no, an' I know him a few year, so I give him a corner until him get better. Damn it! I don't t'ink him is ever goin' to get better. All him do is lie dere an' drink my condensed milk."

"What's wrong with him?" Harry Hamilton asked.

"I dun'no," Stephen answered. "It sound like TB. Boy, him have a cough, you see. But like I did tell you, Mister Hamilton, Captain, him is de real nigger. You know how many time in his life Bargie strike it rich? Seven!" He held up his small, neat brown hands and showed them seven fingers. His vitally good-looking face held contempt and astonishment.

"Seven times Bargie find good stones. One time, dem tell me, de assay office in Zuyder give him five thousand dollar. An' him don't have ten cents leave. If him had been one of my people, now, him would have a big store and a thousand acre of rice."

"And he's really bad sick?" Harry Hamilton asked.

"Lawd, yes, Mister Hamilton. Sick near to death."

Harry Hamilton got up from the long Berbice chair and went to the bar.

"Let me see him," he said, and raised the flap in the counter.

"Sure." There was faint surprise in Stephen's voice, and then he looked at Harry Hamilton with a sudden calculating sparkle in his fine eyes. "Sure t'ing, Mister Hamilton. You ought to see him." He opened the door leading into the storeroom.

In the storeroom it was cool and light, strongly scented with the odours of cheese, brown soap, coffee and salt fish. At the back there was an open window, and the man lay under it in a low-slung hammock. He was dressed in torn, khaki shorts and a roughly darned bush jacket; the red "good luck" sash around his waist was stained and faded. On the floor beside him was a pair of rubber-soled canvas boots, with the canvas of both torn where the swell of the big toe joints had stretched it. The plaited wareshi leaning in the corner by his head was empty except for a rolled-up string hammock, a bush knife and a filthy old felt hat. There was a big enamel mug at his side, with most of the enamel flaked off, showing the dark metal; a wasp had drowned in the dregs of thinly mixed condensed milk at the bottom of the mug. He rested his head on a folded blanket so old that the nap had worn to a greasy smoothness, and he gazed up at Harry Hamilton with hard, appraising and incorrigible eyes.

"Bargie," Stephen said, and the affection in his tone was curious and touching after the sentiments he had voiced outside. "I bring someone to see you. Mister Hamilton from Survey."

"I hear of you, Mister Hamilton," Bargie said, "but we never meet up, eh? How you do, sir?"

"Stephen tells me your chest gone bad on you," Harry Hamilton said. "You sick long?"

"Some little. De rains catch me bad dis trip an' I tek a fever." The weak, panting voice was dry, nearly bored, as if seeking to convey in that laconic assessment the measure of a suave disdain – not bravado nor insensible fatalism, but simply a serene detachment from and contempt for the expected and accessory impotence of what was mere flesh born to distress and treason.

"You got more than the fever, man," Harry Hamilton told him, and as he said this Bargie began to cough, and after a little Buster McKitterick came to the door and gravely watched the writhing, drawn-together body in the hammock, Harry Hamilton took his eyes from Bargie and looked at McKitterick, pulling the corners of his mouth in a downward grimace and shaking his head.

"Man," Stephen said as the last crashing rasp expired, leaving a silence that still seemed to throb with a pulse of terrible sound. "Man, Bargie, you don't have cough; you have devil inside you."

"Bargie," Harry Hamilton said, "you better come with us when we fly back to Zuyder this afternoon. We'll be leaving as soon as the survey boat comes down for the supplies."

"Hospital?" The assured and contemplative gaze was suddenly bleak with caution. Harry Hamilton nodded.

"How long?"

"How the hell would I know?" Harry Hamilton said. "I'm not a doctor."

"All right," Bargie told him. "I better come wid you. I need a little feeding before I go into de bush again."

"Yes," Harry Hamilton said, "you get some good feeding inside you. I think that's a good idea. You want a beer?"

"By Christ, Mister Hamilton, a beer would go good now. T'ank you. Stephen, you don't hear de boss say bring a beer for me?" The long, heavy-jawed death's head was suddenly bright with inspiring and outrageous gaiety as he winked at Harry Hamilton. "All I have been getting from dis damn' coolie is a few crackers an' a little milk so thin you could see de bottom of de mug."

Stephen sniffed, grinned and reached for the mug beside Bargie. "Black people," he said, fondly. "You know, Bargie, if Gawd tek you black people to heaven in a Cadillac, you gwine complain say it not a Rolls-Royce."

Bargie watched the East Indian go from the room with the dirty mug and smiled again at Harry Hamilton, his sunken face burnished with that same shocking and incorruptible gaiety.

"Dat's a good bwoy, you know, Mister Hamilton," he said. "I like tease him a little, but him is a real good bwoy."

Later in the afternoon, when the survey boat had come and gone, the two Indians carried Bargie down from the store. He didn't weigh much, and holding the two ends of his hammock they took him easily down the slope. At the plane Harry Hamilton and McKitterick helped the Indians to ease the hammock into the cabin and on to the floor behind the two pilot seats. Stephen followed with the old wareshi and the torn canvas boots. He looked sad and lost, and kept rearranging the wareshi and the boots and asking Bargie if he wanted another blanket under his head or another one as cover.

"It can get cold up there, you know, Bargie," he said. "It all right, man; you can have anoder blanket. Captain will bring it back to me nex' time him come."

When the engines turned over he squeezed quickly between McKitterick and Hamilton and jumped from the cabin to the float and on to the bank. McKitterick taxied the plane out of the basin and swung into the current. He opened the throttle, and they went down river very fast and lifted above the forest before they had reached the bluff. The plane banked steeply to follow the river course down to Zuyder Town, and Harry Hamilton could see the clearing and the forest closing around it and Stephen on the bank standing a little way from the others and lifting his hand. Then they were flying north by east down the river and the country was tidy, formal and miniature, like a garden, with a thin blue mist beginning to form among the treetops and close to the banks, and with loops of shining water beyond, as far as they could see.

They reached Zuyder Town just before dark, and McKitterick brought them in low over the line of lights along the waterfront and on to the basin. Bargie was sleeping, and he didn't wake even when McKitterick taxied the plane in from the middle of the basin and ran the floats up the wooden slipway that led down from the jetty.

Harry Hamilton opened the cabin door and jumped down on to the wet, smooth boards of the slip as the mechanics came running to make the plane fast for the night. He went quickly up the slip along the jetty to the telephone in the landing office and called the number of his home.

"We've just got in," he said to his wife. "Can you come for me now?"

"Yes, darling," she said. "I'll be there in a few minutes."

"Is Marie with you?"

"Yes."

"Good. I thought she might be. Ask her to come, too. I want her to have a look at a man we brought down."

Two of the mechanics were carrying Bargie up the jetty from the plane. He was awake now, and as they laid him on the bench along the wall of the office he raised his hand in greeting to Harry Hamilton.

"Man," he said, "dat's de best sleep I catch in a long time. I must buy me an aeroplane."

"How're you feeling?" Harry Hamilton asked him.

"Great, Mister Hamilton. A little more rest like I just have an' I'll be back on de old form."

"Good," Harry Hamilton said, "I've asked a doctor to come down and have a look at you. She'll see about getting you into the hospital."

"Doctor is a woman?"

"Yes. She's very good. She's my doctor."

"Oh. Well, if you say so, Mister Hamilton, I'll tek it dat she good."

Harry Hamilton's wife and Marie Rau arrived in Marie's car a few minutes later, and Harry Hamilton, his wife and McKitterick sat in a corner of the office while Bargie was being examined. Then Marie Rau joined them.

"What's the verdict?" McKitterick asked her.

"What do you think?" Marie Rau said. "Galloping consumption is only the most obvious. There's a lot else, including a rheumatic heart. I'll get the hospital to send down for him now."

She picked up the telephone, and Harry Hamilton went back to Bargie.

"She says you're pretty sick," Harry Hamilton said.

"I did guess so, Mister Hamilton."

"You have anybody you want me to tell about you?"

"No. Is I alone now."

"If you go back to the interior," Harry Hamilton said, "it's going to kill you."

"What place don't kill you?" Bargie asked him.

"No, listen," Harry Hamilton said. "I can get you a job in Zuyder when you come out. Come and see me down at Survey, and I'll find you something there."

"I will keep you in mind, Mister Hamilton,"

"That's about all you will do," Harry Hamilton said. "Keep me in mind. Well, remember that I warned you, eh? Remember that I gave you good advice."

"I'll remember, Mister Hamilton," Bargie said. "I know dat you have to do it. As duty."

From the yard beyond the office they heard the soft clanging of the ambulance bell.

"I'll come and look for you," Harry Hamilton told him.

"Yes, Mister Hamilton, you do dat. I sorry we never meet up before."

When the attendants came into the office with the stretcher, Bargie began to cough; by the time they had taken him to the door he was contorted with his furious search for breath. Harry Hamilton was very sorry to see him reduced like that before the women, and to see the passive and aloof self-sufficiency of that battered face now broken by a mindless struggle. He knew that the genial arrogance of that face had been earned without illusions or self-pity, but with a prodigal, debonair commitment of all endurance and all resources; and listening to the sad, racked sounds as the attendants dispassionately closed the doors of the ambulance, he felt warm with anger and shame.

That night after dinner he sat with his wife and Marie Rau on the verandah above the garden in which, since he could no longer go to the interior, he had begun to spend a great deal of time. His house was on the edge of town, by the sea wall, and they could hear the sighing of the tide as it rolled across the mud flats and the soft crash of waves against the stone; the voices from the road by the wall were filtered into murmurs by the hedge of Barbados Pride which he had planted along the fence and which had grown high during the last year.

"But, Harry," Marie Rau said, "he can't go back to prospecting. I don't think he'll ever leave the hospital, myself, but even if he does, he could never survive another month in the bush. Doesn't he know how sick he is? Didn't you tell him?"

"I told him, all right," Harry Hamilton said. "At least, we exchanged formal advice and polite acknowledgement. Neither of us was taking it very seriously."

"You ought to be ashamed. You ought to know better. Do try to do something. I think you actually want that poor old ruin to go back and kill himself, Harry."

"I don't want him to. I simply know that if he can walk, he will."

"But why, Harry? For what? For a few diamonds he knows he'll never find now, and will never live to sell if he does find them."

"Oh, no, Marie," Harry Hamilton said quickly. "It's not like that at all. The diamonds are important, but they're only a part of it. Only a sort of means, really. A justification."

But how to tell it? he thought then, as he looked at the doubtful faces of the two people he loved most in the world. Is there any way of communicating it to those who have never experienced it? Who never, from the shabby confines of this coast, will understand that it is there to be experienced. Will never understand that we are lost without something like the interior. They see only the gains. Bargie's diamonds, the gold dust and manganese, the cattle from the savanna. The least part of it. A reminder merely. Necessary tokens, because we forget easily, of what has been endured, contemplated, promised: the reassurance that immemorable nostalgias of the spirit will be made real finally. The ancestral heritage greater and more precious than anyone race or one history or one hope. Too intense and too real to be encountered directly. Only to be seen from the corner of the eye in the way that the Indians are born knowing, that Bargie learned, that I was learning. How to tell it, my God? And how to tell that it will be perceptible in our later isolation as the elusive, half-remembered fragment of some enormous, receding and unpossessable dream?

The Wind in This Corner

1

In the middle of the morning we drove out of the low, scrubby Queenshaven Hills and into the Braganza Plain. It was very hot and dry outside, but in the car, going fast with the windows open, the heat was only pleasant: a warm, thick-textured rush of air, smelling of baked brick, and a peppery, grass tang of the deep country. Charlie McIntosh was driving us in his car, the big, always dusty, hard-used Buick that had covered every road in Cayuna bigger than a bridle path; I was sitting behind with my forearms resting on the back of the driver's seat; and Roger Eliot sat beside Charlie.

"Well, it's a good day for it," Roger Eliot said.

"A good day for what?" Charlie McIntosh asked, before I could nudge him to keep quiet.

"A good day for murder," Roger told him. "I don't like committing murder in bad weather. That spoils everything. Don't you think so, Charlie?"

"Cho, God!" Charlie muttered. "You don't have to talk like that, Roger. It's not funny."

His florid, pleasant face was hurt and very Jewish, and as he squirmed in his seat I felt the big car surge forward on a burst of new speed. Charlie always finds comfort and release, in any situation that seems to go beyond his grasp, by driving too fast, or by swimming furiously across a harbour in which there are barracuda, or by getting drunk in a dozen widely separated bars.

"How are the other assassins?" Roger asked and turned to look back past me and through the rear window. "Good. They're still keeping up. We won't have to do all the knifework alone."

"It might help if you shut up, Roger," I told him. "None of us are going to enjoy what we have to do. So why not stop whining as if you're the only one who hates it?"

His small green eyes were sombre and forbidding as they turned to me, and his long, pale, ugly face was too vivid; it had been desolated by a conflict of irreconcilable sadness and resolution. I made a fist and punched Roger gently on the shoulder and smiled. "Go on," I said. "I know what the Old Man means to you. But you think we don't feel it too?" He made a wry, tired grimace of disgust and turned away and looked before him again. We were travelling through the cane fields now, but from the rear window I could still see the hills, close behind us and faded by the long dry season. They were a dusty grey-green, stark and inhospitable under the glowing sky. The other cars were strung out along the straight road: Osbourne's Riley and Douglas's black Jaguar close together, and a good way behind, Dennis Broderick's old station wagon trailing a lot of dirty blue exhaust. The canes were all around us, close packed, tawny with the sun, stretching for ten miles down to the coast, where the sky above the swamps was grey and hazy. The pink earth from the fields was dusted on the black road and, occasionally, as the tyres churned the soft surface, a tickling earth smell mingled with the sharpness of hot asphalt would swirl briefly about the car.

"Do we have time to stop for a drink at Sherwood Bridge?" Roger asked me.

"Sure," I said. "Do you need one?"

"Good God, yes, man! I don't want to go in to him cold. Do you?"

"No," I agreed. "A drink would be a good idea. Get rid of this lead in my stomach. We don't want to get caught up in Sherwood Bridge, though. How long since you've been there?"

"About three months," Roger said. "When I was speaking at the Agricultural Show. But it's Charlie's territory. When were you over last, Charlie?"

"Ten days ago," Charlie told him. "There shouldn't be much to hold us up today. They won't have many new things that need listening to. Besides, it won't be a bad thing for Eugene to show his face. He's been so busy in the Eastmoreland divisions, he hasn't had time for Braganza."

"How's he doing in Eastmoreland?" I asked. "Are we going to win down there?"

"You tell me," Charlie said. "Does anybody ever know how Eastmoreland is going to vote? Those Eastmoreland boys kiss you on Monday and hang you on Tuesday, and nobody ever knows why they do either."

"They're not the only ones," Roger said. His voice wasn't pleasant. It was flat and too precise and full of that angry sadness I had seen on his face. "When it comes to kissing and killing, we're doing all right, aren't we, Charlie?"

I saw Charlie's hands tighten on the wheel. He had big hands, firmly fleshed and virile like the rest of his body, covered with reddish freckles and a thick pelt of fine dark hairs. When he turned his face briefly to Roger, the full red lips were thinly compressed and the heavy bar of his moustache made a melancholy, decisive sweep across his profile. "When we stop at Sherwood Bridge," Charlie said, dead and even, "you can take the car and drive back to town. Tony and I will go on with Eugene. If you don't want to do this, then you can back out now. Do anything you want, but I've had enough. You hear me?"

"Me too," I said. "I know Charlie and me and the rest of us are pretty coarse, Roger, compared with you, but just stop reminding us how sensitive you are, eh?"

The strange thing about it was that we all knew we were trying to get angry with each other so that when we reached the Old Man there would be enough anger left for us to do the job properly.

"Oh, shut up, both of you," Roger said. He passed his hand roughly over his pallid, heat-shiny face. "Let me think what I'm going to say to him. You have any cigarettes left, Tony?"

"Sure," I said and smiled at him as he turned around and took one from the package. "Take it easy, boy. We've given you a nasty job, but take it easy."

"You want me to do it?" Charlie asked. "I'll do it, Roger. It ought to have been me from the beginning. Not you. It was a son-of-a-bitch trick asking you to tell him."

Roger looked at him sideways and gave a warm, harsh snort of laughter. "You know something, Charlie?" he said. "You're a nice old bastard. Only your mother and I know it, but you're all right. No. I'll do it. I have to. If you or Tony or Eugene or any of the others initiated this, it would finish him. When he thinks of the Party and the movement now, it's your faces he sees. All of you who were with him from the beginning, or who went to prison with him during the war. No, you couldn't do it. When I do it, I'll be speaking for the new guard, for the hard young professionals who hope to govern this bloody island after the election. He'll understand that, I hope."

We drove on into the hot, sharp-shadowed plain. Nobody wanted to say anything more. We had said it all too often before this Sunday morning, and no amount of talking had made it any easier.

At Sherwood Bridge we stopped beside the yellow, plastered wall of the Chinese grocery; when we climbed from the car and stood on the gritty pavement, the heat rose from the concrete and enfolded us. The water in the gutter ran slimy and tepid around the tyres of the Buick, and a bright dense glare was flung into our faces from the white-limed wall of the courthouse across the street. The little town had the dreamy, suspended feeling of Sunday morning, and a church bell somewhere sounded thin and lost in the still air. In about a minute the first people began to gather around us, and by the time the other cars turned into the street there was a good crowd on the pavement outside the grocery. Even if only half of them meant to vote for us, it was good to see that so many had collected so quickly.

There was a lot of excitement when Eugene Douglas's grey head emerged from his car, and further excitement when Osbourne and Broderick pulled up. Listening to the voices, I realized that unless the Party did something very foolish, we were in, this time. Even allowing for the fact that this was the Old Man's parish, there was a note of recognition and pleasure in the voices that I had been hearing for the last two months in other districts. It came from something more than the Old Man's personal influence, and we all waited a long time for that sound from a crowd.

We went from the pulsing heat of the pavement into the green, bottle-glimmering coolness of the bar. Yap, the grocer, was standing behind scarred wooden counter and smiling as he saw the crowd coming after us. Everyone was talking at once and somebody put a glass into my hand and Yap looked at me, pointing to a bottle of soda on the counter, and I nodded and he opened it and handed it to me over the shifting heads.

This was the sort of gathering in which you realized how good Roger Eliot was. As I talked to the people around me, I could see him in the middle of his group, very tall, white-faced, that distinctive, bony ugliness, turning from man to man unhurriedly. Each response was certain and intimate, and you knew that he enjoyed this campaigning in the grass roots as most men enjoy being with a pretty woman. This was his gift. Charlie McIntosh had it too, by background training and because being with the crowd made him feel happy, but he would never have the legalistic authority that Roger could turn on in the House like the controlled bursts from a machine gun. In the House, apart from the Old Man, the only person who carried more weight than Roger was Eugene Douglas, and then only because he had more experience and had been with the Old Man from the very beginning. And nowadays, when you sat in the visitors' gallery, facing the opposition benches, and saw Roger Eliot and Eugene Douglas lounging side by side, each with that bleakly exultant, histrionic, barrister's keenness on his face, you realized that Roger was the greater man. He was greater because he was younger and we had given him a party and a machine to inherit. Sometimes I wondered if we had asked too much of him too soon. It seemed to me that a lot of youth and a lot of gentleness had vanished from that intense, tautly preoccupied face while none of us were really looking.

He began to tell a clever and destructive story about the government, and even the men talking with Eugene stopped to listen. I had heard it before but, listening to him tell it, I found myself grinning. It was all very personal and rather obscene, as stories like that tend to be in Cayuna. When he had finished, the laughter crashed around us like surf.

"Den tell me, Mister Eliot," one of the men said – he looked like a cane worker or a small farmer in for the day. "How we gwine do when election come? Who gwine win dis time?"

Roger grinned and pushed him roughly, like a father pushing a grown son with affection. Nobody else but Charlie or the Old Man could have done it in quite that way without patronage.

"Who gwine *win?*" he mocked the man, and appealed theatrically to the crowd. "Who gwine win? You hear him? We gwine win, of course. How you can ask a damn fool question like that, man? Lord, but we getting some milk-an'-water workers in the Party nowadays. Who gwine win?" He clapped the man on the shoulder, hard, and grinned down at him, enjoying what he was doing so genuinely that the man grinned too, with delight and confidence, as the rest had already begun to chuckle and repeat what Roger had said.

When it was time for us to go, the men in the bar came out to the pavement and watched us getting into the cars. They were very pleased that we were going on to see the Old Man, and they waved us down the street until we turned the corner by the Methodist church.

Two miles from Sherwood Bridge, Charlie turned the Buick into a pink, rocky side road. On the left there was a big, dried-out pasture with the Old Man's famous mules grazing on the dusty stubble, along with four lordly jacks and seven swollen mares. In the field on the right there was a stand of heavy maize and another of dense, cool-looking tobacco. Then the road began to rise a little, and there, just under the crest of the hillock, was the Old Man's house, and the Old Man, who must have heard the cars, standing against a pillar at the head of his steps, lifting his hand as we drove into the yard.

"Well, gentlemen," he said, and came halfway down the steps to meet us, "what an unexpected pleasure. Charlie, you young scoundrel, I knew you were coming. But not everyone else."

The great, square, cropped head moved forward on the enormous neck as he squinted into the yard to where Eugene Douglas, Broderick, and Osbourne were getting out of their cars.

"Eugene!" he called as he took my hand and Roger's simultaneously. "I almost didn't recognize you. I thought you must have left the island."

"D.J.," said Eugene and came up and put his hands on the Old Man's shoulders. "How are you? I've been out of town every time you've come up. Things are tight in Eastmoreland and All Souls. We're going to need you in both places before the election. If we don't get at least one set of seats from those two, we might lose again."

"We'll get 'em," the Old Man said crisply. "I promise you that. We have to, eh? We can't lose this time. Twice is as much as anyone can afford to lose in Cayuna. After that you're bad luck."

He stood, still holding Eugene by the arms and smiling at us with the slight half-twist of his lips that, for as long as we could remember, had always accompanied his brief, almost aphoristic lectures on the strategy of practical politics. Each of us there, except Roger Eliot, could have written down about two hundred sentences, nearly proverbs, with which, for over thirty years, the Old Man had taught all he had learned.

"No, gentlemen," the Old Man continued. "We cannot lose this time. Do not even entertain the idea. Now let's go in and spend a proper Cayuna Sunday morning. Good heavens, but it's splendid to see you all like this."

He turned and led us up the broad steps – a short, bowlegged old man, with immense shoulders and a back as broad as a bank door, who yet managed to appear of a height in a crowd of tall men. Always, in the past, when you had bent your head to talk to him you had felt as if he were making the concession. And now, as I watched his stiff-collared, immaculately linen-suited figure between the bright-patterned, fluttering sport shirts and casual slacks of Roger and Eugene, there was still enough of the old demonic authority left to make those two towering men appear somehow slight.

"Mildred!" The marvellous gong of a voice carried through the darkened, cool rooms of the old house. "Mildred, we have guests. Tell the girl to bring ice and all the rest of it. Come, gentlemen. Draw up your chairs here. The wind in this corner is always cool for some reason. Some accident of architecture. On the hottest day it's always pleasant here. I know how you Queenshaven people complain about our Braganza heat. It makes men, though. You need a furnace for a good sword."

He watched us as we drew the wicker chairs into a semicircle on the broad, wooden verandah, and his old, wildly seamed face was firm and glowing with happiness. The huge, deer-like eyes sparkled. Once those enormous, liquid eyes and that compactly massive, squat body had been very nearly irresistible. All over Cayuna, now, you could see men and women, of all colours, with those same brown pools that beautified the plainest face, and with those same sloping, heavy shoulders.

"D.J.," Charlie said, "you have any of that whisky you gave me when I was over last week? Jesus, but that was a whisky, man. Don't give it to these crows. They wouldn't appreciate it. Save it for you and me."

The Old Man laughed, an emphatic, musical, bark. He glared at Charlie with a furious love that became suddenly too naked to witness without embarrassment. From the beginning, he had respected Eugene and Osbourne as nearly his peers, or been fond of those like Broderick and myself, but it had been Charlie who filled his hunger for the legitimate son he had never been able to have. Now there was only his daughter, a grey, plump woman called Mildred, silent and distant like so many country spinsters.

"Any of that whisky?" the Old Man said. "Charlie McIntosh, you're a damned blackguard, as I've always maintained. Gentlemen, that person you see making himself at home on my verandah came here last week and under the pretence of talking Party business filled his gut with over a quart of the whisky I keep for important guests. Mildred, for God's sake, child, where is the drink? You want these poor men to die of thirst?"

He raised his voice to an unconstrained shout and rubbed his hands hard together as if crushing his pleasure to get its essence. Then, as the maid came out with the drinks and Mildred followed her, he sat down. We rose, and Miss Mildred nodded to our greetings with a disdain that we knew was not directed at us personally but at whatever fate or chance had caused men to leave her alone with only a genially tyrannical old father to care for. She saw to the maid as the girl set the big mahoe tray with its load of bottles, glasses and a bowl of ice on the low verandah table. They both went inside again immediately.

"Now," said the Old Man. He was alight with anticipation. Talking and drinking were two of the four or five things he had always liked doing best. He took us all in with one quick, hot glance. "Charlie, my boy, work for your living. Find out what these gentlemen would like and give me a whisky and water. You know how I like it."

"Yes," Charlie said, under his breath. "Five fingers of liquor and the dew off a blade of grass."

"What's that? What did you say?"

"Nothing, D.J. Nothing. Just thinking aloud."

"I hope so. I hope that was all."

I felt the smile on my face become unbearably strained and looked at Roger desperately, begging him in my mind to say what he had come to say and stop this ritual exchange between Charlie and the Old Man. Roger was carefully mixing himself a rum and ginger ale, not waiting for Charlie to help him and not looking at anybody. You could sense the crushing Braganza heat in the bright yard, but the wind in this corner of the verandah was cool and gentle. As the Old Man had said it would be. As I had known it would be. I had sat here often enough. After a long time, Charlie gave me my drink. "Here's to victory, D.J.," I said and lifted my glass.

"I'll drink to that, Tony." He smiled, raising his glass first to me and then to the others. "My God, I'll drink to that. It's been a long time, eh? Thirty years. You boys were in your twenties. And Roger – were you born yet, Roger?"

"Yes," Roger told him. "I was born. I wasn't taking much notice, but I was born."

"My God," the Old Man said again. "Sometimes it seems like thirty centuries and sometimes like thirty months. I used to think I was mad sometimes. Expecting this damned island to want independence. You remember what they called us then? The Black Man's Party. Well, if we never win an election, we can be proud of that. There isn't a politician in the island now who wouldn't like to have that title for his party. That's our doing."

"You know what the government boys have started calling us these days?" Eugene asked him.

"No. What?"

"The White Man's Party. I heard Gomez saying that over in Eastmoreland the other day."

The Old Man threw his head against the back of his chair and laughed. The wickerwork gave that peculiar shushing creak of cane as the chair shook under him. "Why?" he asked, and chuckled.

"Oh, because of Roger, I suppose. Charlie, too, if you count Jews. Mostly because Fabricus is standing in Eastmoreland and is being very popular. It's his old parish, you know. Before he came to Queenshaven. He's beginning to frighten the Government now, so Gomez decided to use his colour against him."

"Lack of colour, you mean," the Old Man said with delight. "Good. That's what I like to hear. Black Man's Party. White Man's Party. Jew Man's Party. Chinaman's Party. They'll soon run out of labels. Each time they clap another one on us, it means we're hurting them somewhere."

"We've got them running, all right," Charlie said, "but it's going to be close."

"Close!" the Old Man said. "Of course it's going to be close. But it's our election. I can smell it. If we get in this time, and the next, we're set for a long inning. Good God! After thirty years' fighting, to sit with men like you on a government front bench."

He leaned forward and gave his empty glass to Charlie. The stretched, deeply grooved skin of his face was burnished with the drink he had just taken. Charlie mixed him another quickly, and he leaned back again. The long stomach was quite flat under the gleamingly starched linen waistcoat, and in the irreducible, worn bronze of his face the eyes were much too young and adventurous.

Now, I said to myself, now, Roger. He's given you the cue. Say what you have to say.

I heard the shallow heave of Eugene's breathing beside me. Broderick's fat yellow face was beaded with little unattractive drops of sweat. Charlie was a still, untidy heap in his chair, and Osbourne had begun to finish his drink in small sips.

"Look, D.J.," Roger said. "We haven't come out just to finish your liquor. We want to talk a few things over with you. Election business. And about afterwards." His precise and resonant lawyer's voice was a little high. He looked into his drink, then swallowed half of it.

"Of course," the Old Man said. "I have a number of points I want to raise myself. I shall be putting them before the executive, officially, when we meet in Queenshaven next week, but so many of you are here this morning that I'd like to discuss them now."

"What we had in mind –" Roger said.

"I made a memorandum," the Old Man said. "Mildred was typing it for me last night. I'll go and get it. Gentlemen, your glasses are empty. Charlie McIntosh, you dog, see to your duties or I'll cut you off without a shilling."

He stood up and his stiffness in getting from the chair was barely perceptible. And then we were looking at each other and listening to the slow, decisive footsteps going across the wooden floor of the old-fashioned drawing room.

"He never even listened," Roger said. "Has he ever listened? He's run this damned Party so long he thinks it's his personal property. There's no easy way out of it now, Eugene. I'm going to give it to him straight. He won't understand it otherwise."

"He *was* the Party," Broderick said sullenly. "He was all the Party this island had when you were still wetting your pants, Roger. When I was half your age, he was burning up Cayuna like a bush fire. He has a right to say his say. More right than any of us. My God!"

Roger turned on him with the speed of a biting dog, and I could almost touch the relief and eagerness with which he fastened on a cause for anger, on the excuse for any heat that might drive him through what he had to tell the Old Man.

"Right, Broderick," he said. "You do it. Or don't let's do it. Just as you all please. Say the word, gentlemen, and I'll stop where I started, and we'll listen to what he has to say, as we always have –" He was shaking with desolate rage.

"We'll listen," Eugene said quietly. "We'll listen as we always have. And we'll learn something, as we always have. But not until you've told him he can't stand for election again, Roger. Not until you've told him that he has to leave the House. That's what we came out here for, and you are going to do it, aren't you?"

"Yes," Roger said, and the word was rough with the violence of his conflict. "Yes, I'm going to tell him what he should have realized for himself. But I don't want any of you old comrades in arms looking at me as if it's all my idea."

"Nobody is doing that," Charlie said heavily. "Just do what you have to and get it over. It's going to be kinder that way." Then we heard the Old Man's emphatic footfall coming back across the drawing room. He stood in the doorway studying two closely typed pages of foolscap, his rolled gold spectacles pushed up on his forehead. God knows why the Old Man had ever worn spectacles. His vision hadn't altered much between the ages of seven and seventy-five. But he wouldn't read the posters on a wall without an elaborate performance of taking out the ancient, faded morocco case, removing the spectacles, putting them on carefully, and then, as carefully, pushing them up his forehead, almost to the hairline. This had become part of his legend. Cartoonists used it. Little barefoot boys in the street acted it. Visitors to the House stayed to see it. It hadn't done us any harm at all.

"Gentlemen," the Old Man said, "I was considering our tactics the other night. I feel that we are going to need more emphasis in the North. Much more than we've given it up to now. It has always been our weak spot, and we've always dodged it. Not any more though, gentlemen. We're going to take the fight to them —"

"D.J.," Roger said; his voice was calm, now, and weary, but suddenly assured. As he sat there, leaning forward with his elbows on his knees and holding his glass in both hands, I could see two hectic smears of colour along the cheekbones beneath the very pale, normally waxen skin. "D.J., before you get on to the general plan of the campaign, there is something we'd like to discuss. It's very important."

The Old Man looked up, the frowning flicker of his impatience merely suggested within the lustrous vitality of his eyes, like the lightning you thought you saw behind the mountains at night. "Certainly," he said to Roger. "We have all day. You're staying to lunch, by the way. I've told Mildred. What's come up, Roger? You sound worried." He sprawled easily, in that long-familiar slouch of confident readiness, his face tightening into the still, sharply edged cast of experienced attention, the face of an old hunter to whom any problem is a repetition of one known long ago, and yet one needing care because some detail is always new. "Elections!" he said happily. "They always bring more trouble than any blasted thing I know. Even women. They're the price we pay for being politicians."

"D.J.," Roger asked him, "have you ever thought of giving up the House? Giving up parliamentary work, I mean, and using yourself on the trade-union side?"

"Giving up the House?" We sat in a sort of hypnotized absorption as we watched bewilderment and then exasperated dismissal of an unworthy waste of time struggle for place in the Old Man. "Roger, boy, what the hell are you talking about? If that's what's on your mind, I'll settle it right away. No. I've never thought of leaving the House." He gave a short bark of laughter, half annoyed, half indulgent. "Not until the people of Braganza Parish vote me out, at least. And they've been sending me up for thirty years now. What in God's name brought this on?"

"You," Roger said. "And the elections. And thinking about you after the elections."

"And what I'd be doing in trade-union work at my age," the Old Man said, ignoring him still with the same wry anger that was no more than the quick reflex of a stallion at stud, "I don't know. What's the matter, has Brod been neglecting his duties there?" He winked at Broderick, who was the leader of the trade-union congress that during the years had grown into affiliation with the Party, and Broderick grimaced back at him stiffly as Roger got to his feet. He stood deliberately, and the three steps he made along the verandah and the three steps back were deliberate also, controlled, and almost pensive, and when he stood above the Old Man I thought, Merciful heavens, he looks just like the Old Man did that afternoon during the war when they came to arrest him for sedition as he left the House. And it was true. Roger, as he stood there, was invested with the same moment's quality that I had seen on the Old Man when they arrested him, a quality at once angry and serene, passionately implacable with the sense of utter conviction.

"D.J.," Roger said. "Will you listen?" And the Old Man looked up quickly as the weight of that charged voice roused in him his first serious apprehension. "Yes," the Old Man said. "Go ahead, Roger."

"We're asking you to resign your seat," Roger said. "To resign and not make it an official executive matter. We want you to join Broderick in the trade unions and do the sort of field work you still do better than anyone else. The executive wants you to present them with your resignation when you come up next week."

"The executive," the Old Man said. "I didn't know the executive . . ." His voice had become thick and uncertain, and when I saw the papers in his hand begin to shake I looked away. I didn't want to look at the others. "The executive," the Old Man said again, astonishment – not protest, but stark incomprehension – lending strength to the uncertain voice. "Why? I must have a reason for this." The great eyes, as they stared at Roger, were dulled, opaque and absolutely still, and his face had a livid rigidity, as if he had gone beyond a point of disbelief to where the personal shock was much less than a sense of awed encounter with some fathomless and abstract phenomenon. "Why?" he demanded.

"Because we are going to win this time," Roger said, "and you could not stand five years as chief minister. No, listen, D.J. Let me finish." He was pleading and anxious now, hurrying what he could into the destruction we had chosen him to commit. "Do you have any idea what we're going to have to do in the next five years, after we get in? What sort of mess we have to clear up? There's five hours' paperwork a night for any minister. Let alone the business in the House during the day. Half the year we'll be beating around Europe and America raising capital investment. Off one damn plane into another, living out of suitcases, fighting it out at an all-day conference for an extra million dollars. Do you really think you could do that, D.J.?"

The Old Man's gesture was unthinkably distant and disinterested. "I believe," he said conversationally, almost absently, "that I have proved my capacity for work in the past. Go on. I should like to hear this to the end."

His gaze travelled to each of us, with a flat, bleak absence of surprise that was far worse than recognition of treachery. It was then, I think, that the necessary, hungrily sought anger that had eluded Roger all morning finally seized him.

"Listen!" he shouted. "Listen, D.J.!" Not pleading and anxious now, but shivering in an ecstasy of inextricable rage and sadness. "You can't do it. You know you can't do it. However much you want to. It's a government you'll have to lead in October, not a radical opposition. You'd last a year, maybe two, and then you'd have to go. And even then you wouldn't have done your work properly. Well, we're not going to waste you like that, you hear? What you started in this island and what you built with us are too good to throw away. We want to use you where you'll do a job. On the sugar estates or on the wharves, and among the fishermen. That's what you know. That's what you can do standing on your head. Tell me that isn't so, if you dare."

"I don't agree," the Old Man said.

"You don't agree." It was hard to tell whether the rasp in Roger's voice was savagery or tears or triumph. "Of course you don't agree. Not now. You want to be on the front bench with us. That's what you saw thirty years ago. A front bench with men like Eugene and Charlie and Tony and me. Well, you've got it for us. But it's not for you. And you'll know it tomorrow. You probably know it already, because that's the sort of man you are. If you weren't, do you think I'd be standing on this blasted verandah saying what I've just had to say?"

He was bent over, folded from the waist in that slightly incredible fashion of the immensely tall, whose skeletons seem to struggle for release from the too-scanty flesh; his face, thrust close to the Old Man's, suffused now with the uncontainable mixture of sadness and pure fury, compelling from the Old Man, by some sheerly visible, silent and terrific explosion of will, an acknowledgement not only of those truths by which he had taught us to live in our work but of how well he had taught those truths to us, both men locked and isolated within that explosion of shared service, love and integrity of purpose, neither man conceding one particle of his anger or sorrow or stubborn righteousness, until reluctantly, tentatively, then with sudden and prodigal generosity, the will of the older man recognized the faith behind the will of the younger, recognized that and saluted, also, what it must have cost a man as yet so young and vulnerable.

"Good God, boy," the Old Man said softly, "don't stand there like that. I feel as if you're a tree about to fall on me. Sit down."

Roger sat, in the slow careful fashion of a man who has been exhausted to a point where he dares not trust his muscles to perform the simplest action. As slowly, he took his right hand and a handkerchief from his pocket and wiped the film of damp and grease from his face. He grinned lopsidedly at the Old Man. It was a hot day. Even in this corner of the Old Man's verandah you could feel a declaration of heat, distinct and independent, parasitically attached to the accidental current of cool air.

"I did not realize," the Old Man said, "that this was the feeling of the executive. Of course I shall be proud to accept whatever you may suggest. Gentlemen, your glasses are empty again. There is plenty of time for another before lunch. Charlie!"

His gaze, withdrawn but courteous, roved across our circle, not so much repudiating contact as, for now, impervious to what might mistakenly be offered as a substitute. Passed around us until it rested on Roger, where he sat wrapped in his own exhaustion like a Mexican in his blanket.

Hot, I thought. Dry hot. No rain. Much more of this and the Old Man will have to buy grass from the hills for his mules and his jacks and those mares in foal.

I don't know why this occurred to me then. Perhaps to protect me from an act of intimacy we had all witnessed but from which all but two of us had been excluded.

Living Out the Winter

In Guyana, the East Indians and the Africans between them were tearing the place to pieces. They were doing small, dreadful, useless things to each other all along the coast from the Pomeroon to the Corentyne. The blood of children soaked the pink laterite of the roads, making pungent mud pies in the dust beside the broken shells of school buses tossed onto their sides; old men and their wives drained the last of busy, open lives into the hidden, grey-green waters of the backdams and canal heads; scarlet jets rushed from severed arteries in arcs as pure as rainbows, turned black against the sun, and sprayed the tall blades of sugar-cane and the delicate, lizard-tongue shoots of young rice; the melancholy stench, the grunting and the sobbing of gang rape rose from the ground under the kookorit palms on the horizon at night, rode widely on the wind and made the whole colony drunk with nostalgia for old, exalted cruelties.

It was time for me to go. I had been in Guyana too long this time and there was nothing left for me to do except stay and add my sadness to friends who were sad enough already. There was nothing more to add to what I had already written except more statistics; and the Guyanese were not a people who deserved such a reduction. Over the years, from one visit to another, I had been given more kindness, affection and commodious hospitality here than any traveller had a right to expect. Their manners, their sense of honourable obligation to a stranger, their sweet and courteous exchanges did not belong, it seemed to me, to the age around us but to some fine, archaic inspiration of chivalry. Now, they still took time out from killing each other by inches to press with gentle insistence gifts of food, attention, self on me. As a visitor travelling those violent roads alone between the villages, I was a guest, and my only danger was that in the small, stilt-raised houses I would be forced gradually to drink and eat more than my health could stand.

One afternoon I flew out to Trinidad. The day I left, the Africans decided that single assassinations from the bushes, isolated rape by night and scattered burnings were slow, stingy ways to fight a war. They took out a little township up the Demerara River, opposite the bauxite works at Mackenzie. It was a beautifully planned operation, executed with drastic efficiency. They came in from the forest on three sides just before dawn, burning all East Indian houses from the outskirts towards the river. There was some killing, of course, but more raping because they understood how completely destructive rape is to the East Indian sense of honour. So if I had stayed in Guyana, I would have had a new story full of fresh insights to file.

From Port of Spain, I sent a cable, a night letter, to my wife in London, asking if I could come home now, and two days later she cabled back to say well not now but sometime. This was less than I had hoped for but it was a great deal better than I had any right to expect.

"Don't sit there as if I didn't tell you," Margaret Cipriani said. "You men all think you can play the ass when you have a mind and then just go back as if you have a right. I warned you something like this was bound to happen. Three months ago at this same table. I told you she was going to light a fire under your tail. I know that woman."

All the strength, grace and beauty of our territory rest in the faces of our women, in what they have salvaged and refashioned from the clumsy shipwreck of our past. Their faces are our only certain works of art, and it is to them that we turn for reference and reconciliation.

"Well," she said now, but she smiled as she said it, "what are we going to do with you?"

"I think I'll stay in Trinidad," I told her. "I don't think I want to go to Jamaica just now, and going back to England wouldn't be a very good idea at the moment. I'll stay here."

"You'll stay with us?"

"No," I said. "It looks as if I'm going to be here for a while. I'll find a place of my own before my company begins to wear thin."

"Now you playing the ass again," her husband, Louis, said. "You think I could go to work every day knowing you was staying by a stranger's house and I have an empty room and a place at my table?"

Margaret Cipriani! Louis Cipriani! You hammer such fine shapes out of a man. Between the fire and the anvil of your strong loves one comes sensuously into possession of his special temper.

But all the same, it was time for me to leave the Ciprianis. His poetry was beginning to appear in all the good places, and two writers should not share the same house with one woman for too long. I began to search that day for the sort of place I could call my own until it was all right for me to go home.

In the Press Club one afternoon, Cappie Reckord, a boy who worked for Radio Trinidad, put me on to what sounded like the place I was looking for.

"It will suit you fine, man," he told me. "Feller used to work at Barclay's Bank did stay there. Him and me had shares in a horse, you see, and I pick him up sometimes when we was going out to the track. That's how I know it. It's really a nice place. Your own verandah screened off and quiet, and a big room lead off it so you don't have to use their entrance. My friend transfer to San Fernando last month, but maybe they don't let the room yet. It's a man-and-wife set up. Name of Ramesar. Indian people. At least, him is all Indian, but she have enough black in her to give the leg shape and make the breasts stand out strong. Why you don't give them a ring tonight? Both of them work so you'll have to call them at the house." He paused and winked, with an odd little ducking gesture of his head. All the lewd and cynical disenchantment of Trinidad were in that inimitable wink and nod.

If you live in Trinidad for three days you must learn to resist constant invitations to join an urbane and heartless conspiracy. A frivolous and expert malice is inherited by every Trinidadian like some honorary but unsupported title. "Maybe it's more than board and lodging you get." Cappie Reckord said. "The woman stack – and that little dry-foot coolie she marry to don't look as if him can begin to give her the Vitamin C. I see her a few time when I call by there. Jesus! What a poum-poum going to waste! God never in this life build another race of woman like the real *douglah*.

When my friend was there him tell me that she was always coming into the room to ask him if the maid change the sheets, or if him need a clean shirt for the morning. That sort of thing. Wearing one of them wrap-around housecoat so short that you can't tell whether it's pussy or black panty showing under it when she sit down. My friend tell me that if him wasn't fixed up already and getting all him want, him would have try a shot – but the little Chinese gal him was going with at the time would have take the strength out of the Jolly Green Giant so he just leave well alone. Man! If you get that place and play it right, life could be beautiful."

"All I want is a cheap, quiet place where I can work," I told him. "The beautiful life is a complication I can do without."

"*Eh-eh!* Listen to the man, though. You live in England so long corruption setting in. It's a good thing you decide to take a cure down here before the English brainwash you past redemption."

Because of what Cappie Reckord had suggested about the Ramesar woman, I nearly did not telephone them that evening. A disappointed, indiscriminate wife, an anxious perhaps angry husband, both under the same roof with me, represented the last situation I wanted just then; the first one with which I would be unable to cope. I was near enough to a straitjacket as it was, but I had enough left to know what would make a certainty out of a possibility.

Then it occurred to me that cynics like Cappie are, at best, gamblers. They bet on the worst always coming up and half the time they are right. But only half the time. And their bets are only blind plunges: not based on really careful consideration of form. That evening, after dinner at the Ciprianis, I telephoned the Ramesars.

The house up in Saint Clair was everything that Cappie Reckord had promised: a high-ceilinged, turn-of-the-century, Port of Spain fantasy with deep, encircling verandahs and dark wooden floors. It had a preposterous, ramshackle charm; some festive, slightly askew imagination had conceived it; and half-hidden behind the luxuriant mango and poui trees, it looked more like a big, crazy tent than a sober frame of wood and stucco. My room was at the back, opening off the end of the eastern verandah. Two walls of stout latticework, painted green, enclosed my end of the verandah and separated it from the rest, giving me what was really another room. There was a little door cut into the latticework facing the yard above the steps; and sometimes at night when the winds spilled down from the north-east, the green, cool fragrance they rifled from the huge lime tree across the driveway made my head spin.

The Ramesars had accepted me as their paying guest with a flattering enthusiasm.

"Not the *writer*?" Victor Ramesar had asked me over the telephone after I had given him my name.

"Yes," I said. In those days, I still inflated slightly when a stranger had heard of me and got excited about contact.

"Well, well, what do you think of that, eh? You been writing some great books, man. Just what we need in the West Indies. Our own people writing from the inside about *us*. I saw in the paper where you was visiting, but I didn't know you were going to stay."

"I won't be staying all that long. About three months, I should think. Perhaps that won't be convenient for you. Letting for so short a time, I mean."

"No, man. Don't give that a thought. If you like the place and want it for three months, we'd be proud to let you have it."

And Mrs Ramesar, Elaine, said much the same thing later, after I had seen what they were offering and told them how much I liked it.

We sat in the big drawing room and sealed our agreement over a drink.

"I only got rum, man," Victor Ramesar said, with a touching shy apology, as if he felt he were causing *me* embarrassment by his inability to offer something expensive. "I know how you can lose the taste for it after you live in England."

"Rum is fine," I told him. "At English prices, I haven't been able to acquire a taste for anything except beer and wine."

"Whisky high in England, eh?"

"Wickedly high. Rum too. Sometimes in the winter I break and treat myself to half a bottle, but it's only when I come back to the West Indies that I don't feel sinful about taking a drink."

He brought my glass over, the dark Fernandes rum looking oily and potent around the ice, and I held it while he splashed a little soda into the liquor. Then he went back to the side table and mixed two more drinks and brought them back to where we sat. He handed his wife one and raised his glass.

"Here's to a happy association," he said. "Well, well! I never thought we'd have a famous writer staying under our roof. I read all your books, man. And Elaine here, too."

"Thank you," I said, and raised my glass also. "But I'm not a famous writer. I'm just one of a lot of writers trying to get famous. I'm sure I'm going to enjoy it here. You've got a beautiful house. They knew how to build in those days. The bungalows they're putting up now are just boxes to sleep in."

"If I tell you what this house cost me to keep up, man. It was right for the old-time people when you could get a girl to clean and polish floor for a couple dollar a week, but now a place like this is just a damn white elephant. Me daddy did take it 'bout ten year ago for a bad debt, and when him die him leave it to me. If I could get a price for it, I'd sell it tomorrow and buy one of them bungalow you was talking 'bout."

Looking around as he told me this, I could believe him. Their furniture – vaguely and synonymously Scandinavian, not quite comfortable, slightly depressing with its standardized gaiety and self-conscious modernism – was solid enough; but it was not big enough and there was not nearly enough of it for the space. No juggling could have made it adequate, and Elaine Ramesar had done the sensible thing and arranged the pieces in only one section of the big room. I could understand, also, why they needed to let a room to a congenial boarder, although they were both working and there were no children. The house had not been painted for a long time, and some of it was not used at all; but those floors had to be kept polished and the shingles replaced if he hoped to sell it at a good price to government for offices, or even to some speculator looking for a site, who would pull it down to build high-rise, air-conditioned apartments. And the rates on the half-acre of dankly prolific Trinidadian soil on which the house stood would be a lot more than he would want to meet every year. To keep the jungle from the steps and the house from erosion, he was probably paying out in part-time wages enough to buy food for twenty men, women and children in Port of Spain each week. My contribution, small as it was, would be a relief.

With the move to the Ramesars, my life seemed to acquire, if not a serenity, at least an order that had been missing from it for too long. In the mornings after they had gone to work, I would have breakfast on my end of the verandah, and then I'd sit down to the book that had been a troubling, no, frightening, tenant inside me for nearly two years: a surly demanding invalid for whom I had performed innumerable small and exhausting services every waking hour, who frequently and petulantly called me from sleep, and who resented even those visitors who whispered and walked on tip-toe. Now, and suddenly, it was still a demanding guest, but vigorous and competitive, challenging me to use all the things I had learned, exhilarated by company. At lunch time, I would stop where I knew that I could have written another sentence, maybe even a whole paragraph, which would satisfied me next day, and drive round the Savannah in the beat-up second-hand Minx I had acquired, down to Frederick Street to Luciano's to eat a great deal of oysters and brown bread and drink cold Guinness. The swamp oyster of Trinidad is about the size of a man's thumbnail and its flavour stands in the same relationship to that of any other oyster in the world as the taste of the strawberry does to that of any other fruit: doubtless, I mean, God could have done better in both cases, but doubtless God never did.

After lunch, three or four times a week, I would go to one of the cinemas for a preview. Writing a film column for the Sunday paper was one of the freelance jobs I had landed. The other was a twice-weekly commentary on the international news for Radio Trinidad; and the afternoons I didn't go to the cinema, I would record at the studio. Jobs paid only what such jobs do in the West Indies, but they gave me the rent and my basic food, and I tried to write them as closely and well as if I had been doing them for the *Times* and the BBC. Nobody, as far as I could gather, except for friends like the Ciprianis, read what I thought about new trends in the film, but a number of people would tell me how much they had been impressed by the things I said about de Gaulle and Castro and Kennedy (the one who was still a year away from the underpass in Dallas) and the Middle East.

In the evenings, I usually went back to the Ramesars for dinner; eating with them if they were in; having the maid bring it out to me on a tray if they had eaten already or been invited out. Sometimes if dark caught me still in town I would go out to the Ciprianis in Petit Valley and take pot luck with them, or go to a little Chinese restaurant where you could get a pepper steak and a beer for a dollar.

The nights that I did not talk out with Louis Cipriani, until two or three in the morning, our attempts to rescue a few enduring metaphors from our starved, appalling past, there were parties: loud, loose accidental Trinidadian parties to which everybody comes like a casual Columbus, ready for treasure, astonishment and new delights of the senses.

Most nights I was home early and would read until very late and go to bed with the scent from the lime tree coming through the lattice across the verandah and into the bedroom through the old-fashioned double doors which I never closed. One afternoon there was even a letter from my wife waiting for me: a dispassionate and sometimes sardonic missive, to be sure, but there were seven pages of it, and reading between the lines I could sense friendliness; yes, friendliness definitely kept breaking in. It was not enough, yet, for me to push my luck by going home but things were looking up.

So why did I then allow the Ramesars to intrude on what had begun to come to me more by good luck than any sensible management on my part? Because they both made the house such a good place to live and work in, treating me not like a friend, which would have involved me in all sorts of tedious obligations, nor financially expedient stranger, but as a member of the family: a distant undefined cousin by marriage who was temporarily claiming his share of living space and paying his way? Well, partly because of that, I suppose. You won't really understand us in the West Indies until you understand our habit of adopting into some sort of kin relationship whoever sleeps under your roof for more than a couple of nights. The sociologists call it the "principle of the extended family", I believe – but it stems, simply, from the fact that to be a West Indian is a damned lonely business and that we are always looking for ways to alleviate our loneliness.

But it was not only this that accounted for my growing and often painful involvement with the Ramesars. I had begun to like them; and what was obviously happening to their marriage was what had nearly happened to mine; and with that fatuous, light-headed gratitude of one who has been rescued from a long, dark fall into sadness I wanted to make some sort of return; to somebody. I felt I owed the world a service.

When I say what was happening to their marriage was what had nearly happened to mine, I don't mean, of course, that the details were the same. They never are. The brute weapons with which a man and a woman try to destroy each other haven't changed since we first started recording the business for the guidance of our children; and the strategic aim has always been the same too, I guess. Total annihilation. Even the few tactics we have evolved are so old as to be by now almost ritual. But the terrain is always different, as are the uses made of it; and the occasion that causes the war. All of which has been very good for the writing trade.

With the Ramesars, the occasion was so conventional as to be almost trite: Victor Ramesar was perhaps the least ambitious, most uncompetitive man I had ever met. Most men dream of taking a little revenge on the world for cheating them at birth, but Victor was grateful for the few modest gifts with which he had been started in life: gentle, fine-drawn good looks; a mind competent enough to take him into the administrative ranks of the civil service before he was forty (to a position from which he would never rise, nor even try to rise); a spirit that not only enjoyed the superior achievements of others but was consoled by them; a mild but utterly pervasive conviction that every person was a potential friend to be nourished; an equally mild, equally pervasive conviction that to demand more or to strive for it would be greedy and might involve him in cruelty. With a better mind or with a good fire in his liver, he could have been a holy man – at the least, one of those histrionic idealists who want nothing except a platform and an audience to join them in their exhilarating journeys into new thought. As it was, he was simply the sort of husband who after fifteen years, filled a woman like Elaine Ramesar with daily sensations of boredom, contempt and the furious, unforgiving disappointment of the wife who knows she has only herself to blame for not choosing better in the first place.

It was not that she was one of those shallow, insecure women who feels safe only in a marriage of accumulating possessions and the reflected glow of a high-status husband. But she was not the product of a vigorous and aggressive breed. Her father had started cutting sugar cane on the Caroni estates south of Port of Spain at twelve: just another lean-shanked East Indian child without enough protein in his diet to sustain a field mouse, and who, under the molten suns, livid skies and the stooped, unremitting labour of those brutal fields would have shrivelled into old age by forty.

Instead, at eighteen, he had broken caste and race and invested himself in marriage with Elaine's mother, a Negro, the only child of a local mechanic: one of those self-taught, inspired tinkerers, really, who seem able to follow the course energy must take through any piece of machinery in the way a bloodhound can follow a single scent through a forest.

In those days, when the East Indians were still only a generation or so away from their importation as indentured labour, still unsure of themselves, more than a little frightened by the harsh, individualistic Creole society, still *coolies,* there were several such marriages. At least among the East Indian males strong-minded enough to risk the anathema of the Brahmins and to court the Negro women who had come to recognize that in an Indian husband they were pretty sure of getting a permanent partner; one who would leave a wife only if she were unfaithful, and who would take his responsibilities as father and provider with great seriousness.

From these unions came the douglahs: big, heavy-boned hybrids with skins the texture and colour of the icing on a chocolate cake, vivid, troubling faces, and coarse, straight hair like the manes of black horses. Two years after Elaine Ramesar's father married, his father-in-law got drunk at a picnic down at Mayaro beach, swam out too far, and the last they saw of him was his head being carried like a coconut on the swift brown Atlantic stream, out and away towards Africa. This could have been a financial disaster for the daughter and the son-in-law he had left, since all the real capital of the little workshop and garage he had run had lain in the intuitive skill of his big, shapely hands. But the combination of an East Indian husband willing to be advised by a wife with all the traditions and techniques that the West Indian peasant woman has had to learn over three centuries of keeping the family together is not a partnership to be taken lightly. Elaine's mother sold a junior share in the repair side to another Negro man, managed the spare-parts section and did the accounts herself; and with what she had got from the part-sale of the workshop paid down on a used Bedford truck. In this, her husband began hauling dry goods – cheap cloth, pots and pans, zinc sheets for roofing, nails, salt, even second-hand sewing machines – to the small villages that had begun to grow throughout the Caroni district and beyond as more and more East Indians began to acquire confidence in their new society, to increase and to leave the estate barracks.

By getting up at four on three hundred and fifty mornings a year, returning home at nine on three hundred and fifty nights, and by almost prophetic instinct for those occasions when a dollar's credit given today was going to mean two dollars' extra cash purchase tomorrow, he was soon making more for the family than the repair shop. When Elaine was born, twelve years later, they were living in Port of Spain and her four brothers were wearing the uniform of the island's most expensive, most rigorous preparatory school.

In the course of that winter in Trinidad, I was to meet all the brothers: full-fleshed, genial predators who had staked out crucial commanding heights in commerce and the professions between them. One was a dentist, another was in real estate, a third was a solicitor, the eldest, Lloyd, managed what had grown from the second-hand Bedford truck and the little mechanic's shop, that is, the third largest removal business in Trinidad and the Volkswagen agency.

They were, in fact, close in kind and attitude to their in-laws, the Ramesars. Old Budhram Ramesar, Victor's father, had come to Trinidad with the advantage of being able to speak, read and write English, and had never got nearer to the cane fields than the eastern suburbs of Port of Spain. What Victor had told me about his acquiring the house in Saint Clair as payment for a "bad debt" more or less summed up a happy career as an independent speculator working on the fringes of the law until the day he dropped dead of a heart attack while trying to promote a Caribbean trade fair which, had he lived to see it through, would probably have made him several times a millionaire. When his estate was probated, his three sons found themselves with three hundred and seventy-five thousand dollars owing on bank loans and the house in Saint Clair. Victor Ramesar had not been quite accurate when he told me that his father had "left" him the house. It had been given to him as his share of the inheritance by his two brothers who had realized just how much solid return could be wrested from three hundred and seventy-five thousand dollars of outstanding loans by two legatees for whose continuing good health the managers of four banks offered daily prayers.

I met these two brothers, also, during the course of that winter. They would "flash by" occasionally as they both called it – one in a cream

Mercedes, the other in a green air-conditioned Buick – to spend an hour or so. Half-listening to the conversations as words drifted down to my end of the verandah, I began to form the suspicion that their visits were prompted not so much by family feeling as by the fact that Victor, the civil servant, could give them gossip about his colleagues.

Nothing about confidential government matters, of course, but simple, casual information as to who was doing what to whom. The paths of an import permit or a building licence can be made much smoother if one knows which official to play off against the other. They both shared with Victor a fine-boned, small-featured good looks; but where his face was soft and contemplative, theirs had the hard, alert rapacity of hawks.

Sometimes when one or the other of them was there, Victor would come to my end of the verandah and suggest through the lattice that I might like to join them for a drink. There was always whisky then – Johnnie Walker, Black Label, Chivas Regal, Dimple, Haig – whichever of the brothers was paying the visit.

It was with such a father and father-in-law, such brothers and brothers-in-law, that Victor Ramesar had to live out a daily comparison. Elaine had come from a family of doing and disturbing men. And from a family of equally turbulent males she had picked the one who would never make any new impression on the earth whether he tried to do so or not.

All of this is what I am able to organize now. While I was at the Rames-ars, I registered hardly anything more than that something was wrong and that I was sorry for them both.

I was sorry for him because she humiliated him in my presence and he accepted it: sorry for her because she humiliated him in my presence and was allowed to get away with it.

Some of these humiliations were overtly sexual – as Cappie Reckord had suggested. But I would have been a fool had I read them as signals of readiness. The visits to my room in the short housecoat, the attention I was given when we took meals together, the suggestive banter that eluded him were not for me, really.

They were against him. Sooner or later, I was certain, a lover would be brought into the situation, but it would not be me.

I suppose if there had been any money to spare from among the family enterprises, she would have persuaded one of the brothers or brothers-in-law to give it to her to use to make something of him – as her mother had done for her father. But all the brothers and brothers-in-law had sired enormous broods, tribes almost, and there was not enough left over to risk on Victor. His capacity for ruthlessness was too limited. So he continued to initial files at the Ministry of Development, and she to make out invoices and bills for the brother who held the Volkswagen agency.

It would be useless, and tedious, to recite all the other ways in which Victor was reminded, daily, of his inadequacy. An embittered woman looking for some excuse for not loving the decent man with whom she lives can only hope to provoke him into doing something that will confirm how right she has been all the time. And if the man will not be provoked and she is herself also a basically decent creature, what else is there to do but keep repeating the dozen or so cruel yet trivial attacks on his confidence, his integrity, until she comes to believe them?

For Victor accepted her recriminations, her unpredictable gusts of shrill anger, her retreats into wordless sulks, even her obvious use of me with a solemn meekness, a bewilderment that was infuriating. He had never learned what his brothers, and hers, were probably born knowing: that a woman will forgive her man almost anything except a too-humble evaluation of himself.

One early evening after one of the brothers had "flashed by" – I cannot remember whether it was cream Mercedes or the air-conditioned one – there was a particularly distressing quarrel. No, not "quarrel", which implies some sort of heated *exchange*. You could not call it even a "scene". It was just the ugly, corrosive sound of a woman trying to find grievances to justify her rage. She must have been cooking this outburst a long time on a low fire because she did not raise her voice. It was only low-pitched phrases that occasionally ricocheted through the lattice like shell fragments falling on the margins of a battlefield. "*. . . fifteen years an' we right where we started . . .*" "*. . . never do a damn thing but go out to work an' come back to this damn morgue . . .*" "*. . . furthest we ever go is two weeks in Barbados . . .*" "*. . . everybody else have something to remember . . .*" "*. . . not even a damn child into the house . . .*" And so on. The banality of our most profound despairs!

We so seldom have even the bitter sustenance of real tragedy, of dramatic catastrophe to console us.

A little later, I looked up from the letter I was writing to my wife and saw him mooching forlornly under the pomerac trees on the front lawn across the drive. It was only a few days to Christmas and the pomerac was in full flower; against the showy Trinidadian sunset – all hard lemon and furnace red – the pink blossoms were of a not-quite-credible delicacy; and when they floated to the grass in unexpected showers, they stained the air under the trees with a soft blush and powdered the ground like improbable, rosy snow. I wondered if it was snowing in London, and if my wife and the man to whom I had forced her to turn were walking in it. But even thinking this, I found I was feeling sorrier for Victor Ramesar hangheading it under the pomerac than I was for myself.

On the impulse I rose and went to him under the trees. Casually, so as to conceal that I had heard anything (or rather, so as to offer him the courtesy of the lie that I had heard nothing), I asked if he and Elaine would come to the cinema with me that night, as my guests on my press pass. He hesitated, and the big, lustrous, dumb eyes searched me with what in another man might have been suspicion, but which with Victor were only confusion and a sort of appeal. Then he went into the house and a few minutes later came out again to say that Elaine had said yes and thank you.

The evening was not a success. Elaine was still sulking, and Victor was still picking his way through the rubble of guilt or unvoiced protest or perhaps just tired sadness. Whatever it was with which one of Elaine's assaults left him. When we went up to one of the little night clubs in Saint James after the show, they both kept talking at me: he with what, to my embarrassment, I felt was gratitude simply for having rescued him from an evening alone with her at home; she with a bitter eagerness to hear about my life in London, the people I knew, the world of success, variety, glamour. She made so much of the dingy, anxious round that is most of a young writer's life, invested my most careful and dispassionate replies with such brightness, that I began to feel phony. All the small triumphs and exhilarations – being able to make your own hours, subsidized travel, parties where the names of half the guests were sufficient, on introduction, for you to know what they had done, your own name being known by some of those people because it was attached to something you had done – all this became, in the light of Elaine's need to be vicariously excited, something false and tawdry. She was using me again: to prove to herself and to Victor how he had allowed life to pass them by. But this time, I was party to the act of humiliating comparison. That I tried to turn the talk in other directions was not enough; by consenting, however reluctantly, to being drawn, I allowed myself to become the co-respondent in a dismal kind of adultery.

From this evening, the Ramesars and I often went out together. It had been near Christmas when we first became companions of a night. Christmas and Shrove Tuesday, Trinidad gives itself over to pleasure with the exquisite, nervous concentration of a racehorse in the gate. The Christmas and New Year festivities are a warm-up, really, for the serious business of Carnival. All over the island, but particularly in Port of Spain, the preparations begin to accumulate on the morning after Twelfth Night. A tenth of a year's wages will go into the making of a Roman legionnaire's uniform, a Papuan warrior's head-dress, a medieval king's coronation robes, each accurate down to the last sandal strap, the last bird-of-paradise feather, the last tippet of ermine. The public library sets aside a room entirely stocked with volumes on costume through the ages, and prodigious exercises in historical research are undertaken by the bandleaders – men whose schooling may have stopped at sixteen – and are submitted to the Carnival Office in ten-cent notebooks for registration. In the working-class districts, fantastic efflorations are conjured out of dressmakers' scraps, coloured tissue, tin foil, cardboard and added to war-surplus American Navy uniforms bought for a dollar apiece. On the Monday morning before Ash Wednesday, ten or fifteen thousand of these King Sailors turn Frederick Street into a garden bed. The champion calypsonians anxiously tighten the sprung rhythms and file the barbs of the satires they will offer in the tents during the fortnight before Carnival to the most acute and demanding popular audience in the West Indies, maybe in the world. At nights, the drone of the steelbands practising in a hundred yards beats like an enormous pulse under the skin of the city, just beneath the level of conscious listening.

It is a time of parties. Planned parties; informal gatherings that become parties by chance; parties that begin in one house and move across the city to another, coalescing with and dissolving from yet others on the way. And as Carnival drew nearer, the Ramesars and I were increasingly invited out as a sort of family group. After New Year, I had asked the Ciprianis if I could bring them to a big Sunday picnic across the mountains on the beach at Blanchisseuse; and since then it had been more or less assumed that they were with me. In the West Indies, people never like to miss an opportunity for exercising their right to be hospitable, since, for so long, it had been about the only right they could exercise spontaneously. Things are changing now, I suppose, with independence and all, but the habit seems to remain.

And with these invitations among new people, or among people they had known only to nod to, the Ramesars began to end their marriage. They, or at least she, would have ended it anyway, but getting to know the Ciprianis and others was too much for what was left of it too suddenly.

It was not, I must stress again, simply a matter of her wanting vulgar success. Few of us had much money. Not in the way her brothers and brothers-in-law had money. And only one or two of us would have done anything that we did not enjoy doing to get it. But most of the men among whom she was now moving were doing things that not many others could do half as well. You could hear it, as you always can, in the conversation: much of each man's talk being about his trade, and the other men listening because there is always so much to learn about your own craft from somebody else who practises his adventurously. And you could sense it in the attitude of the women: each of them sometimes proud, sometimes exasperated, always proprietorial about having to put up with a man to whom work was not simply so many paid hours to be got through but a way of life.

But I did not realize what our company was doing to Elaine Ramesar at the time. Indeed, I had begun to feel hopeful, a little proprietorial myself, about the marriage. She ceased, almost, to find fault, and when she did it was casually, with more rough teasing than sullen accusation. The brooding sulks lightened, and sometimes the exchanges that came to me in my corner were almost affable, couched in the intimate shorthand of a longstanding partnership.

So that the suddenly emptied house in which I found Victor standing dazedly when I came in one afternoon overwhelmed me almost as much as it had him.

She had taken everything. All that was left was my bed, the table with my books and manuscripts, and the long Berbice chair in which I read at night. She had even had the stove uncoupled from the gas pipe and taken that too. My soiled clothes had been freshly laundered and packed with the others in the two suitcases out of which I had been living for nearly half a year. Victor's fresh linen, suits, shirts, ties, everything lay on the floor of the bedroom as she must have tossed them before the removal men took the wardrobe away. In the little washroom beside the kitchen we found his stale clothing piled in the concrete sink. The maidservant, a big, good-natured slut from Grenada, had been paid off; at any rate she was not there. A note had been left for me on top of the shirts in one of my suitcases. It apologized for any inconvenience I might be caused, but explained nothing. I didn't want to look at Victor, but there was nothing else to look at in the big house that now echoed like a looted sepulchre.

He said, "She can't do this to me," and I waited for what I was certain he would say next, "How could she do this to me?"

There was no way I could tell him, with kindness, that if he had to ask the question he already knew the answer. And it seemed to me he had had enough cruelty for one day.

There was a numb panic in his eyes as he looked about the house she had stripped. A lot of a man is the sum of his possessions; and now, except for the chair and the bed she had left me, he did not have even a place to rest what remained of him.

He sat on the edge of my bed, carefully; on the extreme edge, as though he were apologizing for taking a liberty. There was a little rum left in the bottle I kept for going to bed when I finished reading and I poured him all of it into the plastic tooth mug on the little glass shelf above the washbasin and ran a splash of water into it. There was no ice because there was no refrigerator. I was trying to find something to say as I gave him the drink but just about everything that came to mind seemed empty or patronizing and sometimes both.

"I'm going to kill her," Victor said, holding the drink but not tasting it. "I'm going to find her and kill her."

It carried less conviction than any threat I had ever heard uttered.

"I'm going to sue her," he said next. "She going give me back what she

take or she going find her ass in jail. She can't do this and get away with it."
He looked up at me hopefully.

"Yes she can, Victor," I said with regret. "She's allowed to take everything under your roof if you're not here to stop her."

But he knew that. He was simply stumbling from threat to threat for the
consolation I could not give him.

Then he looked away, down into the drink I had given him, and his
weak, sweet, victim's face blurred and crumpled and he began to weep.

"She could have had every damn thing," he said. "She could have had
the house and everything. But why she had to do this to me? After all the
years I love her, how she could do this to me? Like this!"

And with that, the Ramesars began to pass out of my life. I went back
to the Ciprianis and stayed on since I had got a letter asking me when I
was coming home and knew that I was not going to be in Trinidad much
longer. One afternoon at a wedding, I met a girl, a barrister, who had read
one of my books and who wanted to know me well for a while but who had
no illusions about what knowing me would become. From time to time,
I would go to the big, hollow house in Saint Clair in which Victor was
beginning to reassemble a life. But there was very little to talk about except
Elaine. She was now lodged in the tribal embrace of a brother's family and
they treated with affable, condescending neutrality all Victor's attempts to
see her. It was not that they had anything against him. But they didn't have
anything for him either. He was a loser. And in their world, losers were a
nuisance. Bad luck.

I saw her once after she had left him. She was lunching at Luciano's with
a big Norwegian who flew a crop-dusting service. I had a drink with them
but Victor's name did not come up; and when I next saw him there seemed
little reason to say anything about the matter.

Carnival was now nearly on us, beginning to toss the island between
its paws. At nights, the sound of steelbands thudded in the bloodstream as
in her flat on Saint Vincent Street, six stories above the city, my girl and I
wrapped ourselves around each other like the tails of two kites. In the days
when she was in court, I wrote steadily at her Formica-topped kitchen
table. Just before Carnival I got a letter from my wife telling me that I
was missed, and another wanting to know whether I would accept three

thousand pounds for doctoring a screenplay as soon as I returned to London. Both letters came on the same day.

With all I had going for me then, it was hard to remember or to do much about the tears of an unconsidered man.

Reckonings

*H*is manservant found him sitting up to the desk as he must have died, on the instant, with only the pen falling from his hand in the middle of a word that, from what led up to it, his literary executors were later to decide would have been *now* but which had ended as *no* – the *n* nearly completed at the top of the circle before the spasm in the ambushed fingers had dragged a cracked, thick, curiously decisive stroke three inches down and across the page; the word begun quite near the left-hand margin of the ruled exercise book he always used for manuscript and the last of what must have been already a dead hand's mark not quite crossing the empty line beneath; curved up and away from it, in fact, with a flourish striving optimistically for the right.

This was at a few minutes before or after midnight, or perhaps half an hour to forty-five minutes later. Purcell, the man who discovered him, was only certain of having caught the eleven-five bus at the foot of the hill, travelling fifteen to seventeen minutes in it (few delays at that time of night, at obligatory stops), walking anything between ten and fifteen minutes again up the side road to the house, through the gate and (again) up the drive past the flame of the forest under which the oblong of aluminium shed was set on two-by-two concrete blocks above the lawn: the bent-over, downward-gazing profile he passed on five nights out of seven was suspended in the

---

*Pseudonym on typescript: Angela Saumarez.

pool of light cast by the reading lamp on the desk placed dead centre against the study's one windowless wall.

In bed, however, some intuition of unease, formless but obstinate, kept coming between Purcell and his sleep, and he had finally risen, left the servants' quarters and gone back down the moon-drenched drive, across the coarse grass, and knocked tentatively then with increasing urgency at the study door.

The eight-o'clock news gave Renfrew's death a considerable space of time, but by then his daughter at the other end of the island had been telephoned. "He was born lucky," she said to her nearly brand-new husband as she switched off the small transistor set that stood on the breakfast table between them. "Things always seemed to go right for him. Friends, houses, travel, money, children, recognition. He never *wanted* for anything in his life. Even death didn't break the run. I mean, can you think of a better way to go than *that*," and she nodded at the radio over which the announcer had respectfully summarized the circumstances in which Martin Renfrew had been found dead. "If he had ordered it, he couldn't have been luckier."

He looked at her with a sense of disquiet not far from alarm. Theirs had been a short courtship, given over almost entirely to consummating the desires they had both acknowledged within an hour of their first meeting. Since the marriage, nothing had changed except that their lovemaking had become more intense, frequent and protracted. Now he realized that he knew no more about her than a tourist knows of a city from a Sunday afternoon among the squares, cafés and parks, with the people dressed for the holiday promenade, talking only to fill the spaces between small, bright occasions.

"Deborah!" he said, on a note of careful reproof. "He wasn't only lucky, as you put it. He worked for all the things he got.

"What's wrong with being lucky, anyway? You make him sound as if – as if he was some sort of cheat." Almost sulkily he added: "I thought you loved him."

The wide-set, greeny-blue eyes across the table from him were opened full, in surprise.

"Of course I loved him. What makes you think I didn't?" She sounded impatient. "And I never said he was a cheat. I said he was lucky. Bloody lucky! I don't mean big luck – he never got the Nobel or five million dollars or screwed a Spanish duchess or fathered a genius or anything like that – but just nice steady little bits of luck falling on his head all his life. He was the best insulated son of a bitch I've ever met. Christ! If we have half his luck between us we'll be doing better than most."

"Deborah," he said, anxiously now. "Don't. Take it easy, darling. Don't try to hold it in like that. I know how you must be feeling. It was a shock, getting the news like that in the middle of the night. But let me try to help." He reached across the little glass-topped table at which they were having breakfast and tried to take one of the tautly doubled fists on which she was resting her chin.

For the space of a frown, at once preoccupied and exasperated, she resisted, and then she smiled faintly and let him take her hand and hold it resting on the table beside the shallow bowl of red and yellow hibiscus. Through the glass of the table top he could see her legs, the short house-coat cutting far up her thighs, and the dusting of fine, bleached hair on the deeply tanned skin that always excited him. It excited him now and he tried to put the thought away because it seemed a disloyal, even indecent, thing to be thinking about at the time.

She smiled faintly again, and tossed her chin at him and said, "Lord, but I'm a bitch sometimes. You've been sweet and strong and protecting ever since it happened and I've done nothing but put you down. Forgive, darling?"

"Don't be silly," he said, smiling too, but knowing that for all of the smile and the gentle tightening of her fingers around his, she was only looking at and not into him.

"You're sure you don't want me to come over with you?" he said. "I don't like the idea of your being alone when you're feeling like this."

"No, darling. We've decided that. Of course, I'd love you to come over today, but you know you really ought to be here to meet MacAlpin when he flies in. He's too near buying now for us to blow it. And if you leave that stupid prick Roberts to do the meeting, we will blow it. He'll have to go, you know. Roberts, I mean. He's worse than useless. As soon as we've nailed MacAlpin, we'll have to cut him adrift. We'll be able to afford it then."

"Yes," he said, not happily. "I suppose you're right. I still wish I was coming over with you, though."

"I'll be *fine*, darling." The impatience was plain now beneath the fond protest. "The funeral isn't until Friday and I'll have more help than I know what to do with in making the arrangements. Thank Christ, David was filming in Nassau and not in Hong Kong or some place like that. He'll be able to cope with all the sympathizers. He's coming down tonight."

"Yes," her husband said. "So you said after you rang him." "You'll like him," she went on. "Everybody likes David, and a lot of people adore him. That's what makes him such a marvellous director, I suppose. He's so damned gentle and *interested* that you want to do your best, just to make him happy. You wait and see. After it's all over, I'm going to insist he spends a week with us. He hasn't been home for two years, and two years is a long time without David . . . God, look at the time!"

"And I'm not dressed or packed. Phone the airport, darling, and tell them I'm on my way. They'll hold the flight a few minutes if you ask nicely." She pushed her chair back from the table and rose and walked briskly across the verandah to the doorway leading into the drawing-room. In the doorway she turned, looked back at her husband and gave a sniff of amusement. "You know what's going to be wild?" she said. "The ex-mistresses. There's about ten of them I'm certain of, and a couple more I'll know for sure by this afternoon. They'll all come up to the house to see if I need any help. And they'll all be dressed as if they were thirty instead of seventy because they won't know if any of the others are going to be there. He must have been a real ball of fire. Even when it was dead and finished, they never seemed to give up trying to start something again."

But she caught the ten-thirty flight with time to spare and was in Queenshaven by eleven. Uncle Harold, who was not really her uncle but her father's closest friend, was at the airport to meet her.

"My dear," he said, and held her close. "I'm so sorry for you."

"Hal," she said. "You were wonderful on the phone last night. You must have been feeling rotten and you were wonderful. If I had to get the news like that, then I'm glad it was you."

She kissed him again on his slightly puffy, old man's cheek that smelled of age and shaving water.

"I was in the House," he said. "We were sitting late on that wretched sedition bill. Your father's people were very good. They telephoned me at home and nobody was there. Louise is over at Minden, and we don't keep the servants any more when we're not both in Queenshaven, so they couldn't get a reply. But they rang the House. I think it's damn good that they thought of that. I went up right away and got things going. Called you from there, as a matter of fact. And got young Calder out to do the PM so we could send him straight down for embalming this morning. Louise is coming up today, of course. She's probably at home now. She'll take over on all the details . . ."

He more or less repeated all this as they drove along the Barricades from the airport between the dark blue, satiny swell of the harbour and the bottle green and splintered glass of the Caribbean flinging itself against the exposed shore. Repeated it energetically, as if to emphasize how active he had been since midnight.

But when they reached the house in the hills where she had grown up, he was suddenly very tired, and put up only a token resistance when she would not allow him to get out of the car.

"Take him straight home, Clifford," she said to his chauffeur. "You hear? Don't let him talk you into anything else," and to him, "Now you get a good rest. Understand? I don't suppose you've even *thought* of stopping since last night. I know you. Tell Aunt Louise to come over as soon as she can."

"Shall I send Clifford back with the car?" he asked. "You'll have a great deal to do and you don't want to be driving yourself around all afternoon in this heat."

"Bless you, darling," she said. "But there's the car here and I'll be fine. I like driving. And if I have to keep my eye on the road, I won't be able to do much thinking. Which is just what I want: not to do much thinking today."

"Yes," he said. "I can understand that." Then defensively, as if near to quarrelling: "I told your father to get a cardiograph done. If I told him once, I told him a hundred times. Ask Clifford there. Martin, I'd say, I'm going to have your Calder run a check on me; you'd better come along and have one too."

He had stuck his back deep into the corner of the rear seat of the big,

black car, and when she leaned in to kiss him, he moved his head forward
to meet her lips grudgingly, with a turtle's caution.

"I know, darling," she said. "You always tried to take care of him better
than he'd ever do for himself. You did more for him than he deserved. I
mean that, Hal. You're the best thing that ever happened to us, and I'll
never be able to love you enough for being around when I was growing up."
She nodded, almost imperceptibly, at Clifford's reflection in the rear-view
mirror, and stood back as the car moved off down the drive.

The flight down from Nassau and Jamaica was delayed, but it wasn't going to
be late enough to justify her driving into the Queenshaven suburbs and finding a drink and a meal in one of the many houses that would have offered
her both. So she went up into the air-conditioned lounge that overlooked
the runways and across those and the big harbour to the city and up to the
hills where the house that had been her father's and was now hers was set
among the trees at the head of a sheer, narrow valley. She sat on a banquette
in the corner, and ordered a beer, and hoped that no one she knew would
see her drinking alone before David's flight came in and feel that because
of liking or politeness they ought to keep her company. To look out of the
sealed plate-glass window, she had to sit side-saddle on the banquette, which
meant that she did not have to see anybody who came into the lounge unless
they came right up to her. And what lay beyond the window was all she
wished to see until David's plane came dropping out of the north. Looking
out at the swollen, purpling clouds around the high blue peaks of rain forest
to the east, and then to the pink-edged sky green as an unripe apple over
where her home stood in the bushy, lower hills to the west, she knew that
she would never be able to leave this island and this sea for long. She would
die here, unless she were very unlucky, as her mother, who had come from
England and who had been happy at first, then desperately unhappy, then
happy again, had insisted that she be brought back here to die.

Up at the house, Aunt Louise, who was not really her aunt but Uncle
Harold's wife, would be sitting with the last of the ex-lovers. They had
started coming up, as she had anticipated, soon after she had got in. Not all
of them. Four of those she was certain of could not have wanted to come.
One had telephoned. And at some time when she had not heard of it, two

had died. This must have been when she was in England or America or India. But it must have been when she was in England because that last long time in England was after America and India – and when her mother, because of sickness, could no longer write the trenchant, gossipy, honest letters that hitherto had followed her wherever she went.

She sat and drank one beer, and was halfway through another when the speaker above the bar announced the approach of David's flight.

Watching him cross the wide, naked expanse of floor from Customs, she thought, *My God, it's Daddy. He looks so much like Daddy it's ridiculous.* And then thought that it was ridiculous of her to feel that, since David was her father's son as much as she was her father's daughter and had as much possibility of looking like the man who had got them on different mothers as she. "How's my boy?" she said and bent a little to put her arms around him very tightly, and to put her long, dark head close against his blunt, sandy one. "Did you have a good flight?"

"Hullo, wonder woman," he said. "Hug me a little more. You're the first thing that's felt real since I got the news. Everything has felt so damned unreal."

"Oh, David," she said, "you can't know how glad I am you're here."

Going back along the Barricades in their father's car (both waters silvered black under the moon but with the white spun-glass breath of foam still marking the open sea), David asked her: "What happened, for Christ's sake? I telephoned him two days ago. He was coming up to spend a few days with me before we finished shooting. Just to look at what I'd done and give his opinion. It was my idea, but London put him on the budget as soon as they heard. They hadn't thought of him as being available, let alone as being my father . . ."

"It was a coronary," she said. "You know, the one that hits you before you realize it. He was leaning against the sidewall of that old roll-top of his. That's why Purcell didn't know he was dead at first, when he saw him. He thought he was just thinking and writing."

"Purcell? Who's Purcell?"

"You remember Purcell. *Major-domo* Purcell. The one who's always trying to sell something so he can raise enough money to go to America."

"Oh, yes, *Purcell*," he said. "I remember."

She turned the car into the road that ran round the head of the harbour and into the city across the water from the Barricades.

"Would you like to see him?" she asked. "He's down at the parlour. We could drive straight into town before going up to the house? The parlour will be closed, but there's always someone there."

"No," David said. "I don't think so. There doesn't seem much point, does there?"

"I agree," she said, "but I felt I ought to ask." She turned the car north, away from the harbour, into the first of the suburban roads that would bring them to the foothills. "I'm not going to have any ceremony at home. The body will go straight from the parlour to the crematorium. I've asked Father Aveni to say something about him out there."

"Father Aveni? A Catholic? But he wasn't a Catholic, Deborah. I didn't think he was anything. Or did he get converted since I last saw him?"

"Oh no. Nothing like that. But he was very fond of Father Aveni, and besides – he was very superstitious, you know? He used to say it was bad luck for anybody to get born or married or buried without a priest of some sort taking part in it. He said it didn't matter if it was only a witch doctor shaking bones so long as he was a serious witch doctor."

"No," David said. "I didn't know that about him. I suppose I didn't know much about him at all, really."

She glanced quickly at the blur of his face, and then, with her eyes back on the white splash at the end of her headlight beam, raised her left hand from the wheel and reached across and gently tickled the hollow at the base of his skull.

"You mustn't feel like that," she said. "Not now. You meant a whole lot to him, and he was terribly proud of you. He once told me that everything he'd done in the last ten years was really written with you in mind; to you as reader. That if you liked it, then it must be good."

He took her hand from the back of his head and kissed her fingers and put them back on the wheel.

"Thanks," he said. "You really are a wonder woman. And I'm sorry about the self-pity. It's just that I've felt so unreal since you called and told me. It's as if there are a lot of hollow places inside me that'll never be filled."

Up at the house, Aunt Louise had left a note welcoming David, saying she was tired, promising to come back in the morning; and Rose, their father's maid, had laid the table for two and left a casserole in the turned-down oven.

"I told Rose not to wait," she said. "The poor old thing has taken it hard. She came to work for him before he even met my mother. I didn't want her to do anything for us tonight – I thought we'd eat out – but she'd have felt worse if I'd suggested that."

"Now I know I'm back in Cayuna." He smiled at her from the doorway between the pantry and the kitchen: a slight, sandy, open man with the unlit patches of an irretrievable sadness in the depths of his eyes. "D'you realize how anachronistic what you've just said sounds? Faithful retainers grieving for their old master. In this day and age. Don't you West Indians ever change?"

She grunted over the loaf of new bread which had been left to cool on the counter and which she was now slicing. "We've changed, all right. Rose is one of the last. *I* won't have anybody like that after she goes. That's all over. In a few more years it'll be just like England or America."

"That's what your mother told me," he said. "When I first came out, twenty-two years ago. When you were about two. No, you weren't two yet. I remember you used to start walking at the top of the driveway and not be able to stop until you reached the bottom because it was so steep. Your mother used to stand at the top, laughing, and I'd be at the gate with my heart in my mouth, thinking you were going to fall and really hurt yourself. I think that's when I decided, seriously, to be a director and not an actor. Just to capture and to share what it looked like to see you tumbling down the drive with your mother laughing at the top all of a sudden seemed the most important thing I could do."

She turned from the counter, with the half-cut loaf and slices on a board in one hand and a bowl of salad in the other and butted him in the chest with her shoulder to clear her way through to the pantry.

"I remember," she said over her shoulder as she went through to the dining room. "I remember you at the bottom of the drive. You looked huge. You looked bigger than Daddy. For a long time after you went away, I couldn't get used to the idea that you weren't going to be there at the gate to catch me. I couldn't remember your not being there."

After they had eaten, they sat out on the verandah above the sudden, dark drop of the valley and the brilliant smear of the lighted city across the plain. At this distance, and from this height, the harbour was a dark space behind the city's glare and the open sea beyond the Barricades showed itself only in long glints as the Caribbean lifted against the moon. They lay in the long Berbice chairs their father had once brought from Guyana, and put what remained of the last bottle of brandy their father had bought between them.

"It has been a long time," he said. "The last time I saw you, you were still a girl, really. Still my small sister. Now you're a woman." And then, "I wish I could have come when your mother died, but it was impossible."

"I know," she said. "It would have been wonderful if you could have come, but you couldn't. Your letter almost made up for your not being here, though. Usually letters don't help much at a time like that, but yours . . . I hadn't been able to cry at all; it was all locked up inside like some horrible weight that didn't belong to me. And then your letter came and I cried it away. I didn't realize you knew her so well. All the things you said about her were so true. They were exactly what I had been trying to say to myself but couldn't find the words for. She seemed to be slipping further and further away because I couldn't find the words and I was getting terribly frightened that I'd eventually have nothing left. Then your letter came and I got her back."

"I didn't know her all that well," he said, "but I knew what she had done for me. I was in a pretty bad way when I came out that first time, you know. It wasn't just trying to become a son to a man who had left my mother and me before I could even remember his face. It was a whole history of confusions; of growing up in England with a ghost in Cayuna nobody would admit was part of the house, but who had to be acknowledged some time. An accumulation of foolish, well-meant, utterly disastrous attempts to do the best for me. Like his not being allowed to write to me or send me anything while I was growing up – when his name kept blowing under the door in reviews, or when one of his plays was on television. We even had one of the short stories, once, in an anthology at school, and the boys teased me because the surname was the same as mine and I didn't know how to admit to them that Martin Renfrew was my father. So I simply played along with the teasing and pretended that he had nothing to do with me, and went home that afternoon feeling as if I had killed him before them all. No, not killed him. That would have been bad enough. Wounded him, rather, and left him bleeding and helpless. Or like the time when one of the men my mother married – the second-to-last one – wanted to adopt me legally and they had to write to my father to get his permission. Thank God that English law is based on such a strict sense of property and inheritance. They could have disposed of me, of *me* and my name, just like that, if they hadn't had to get my father's agreement. One stupid woman and a jealous bastard who only wanted me to have his name because it was beginning to look as if I might do something that his own son couldn't. I think that when my father refused to let them adopt me, I really knew *I* was me. I don't know what instinct prompted him, but it was so right. The day his letter came saying *no,* I began to live. That was the day I knew I had to see him again. But I wouldn't have been able to make it when I did if it hadn't been for your mother. She made it between us. She set herself to make it between us. All the time I was here, when you were only two, she treated me as if I were my father's son."

"That was her speciality," she said. "The first question she asked herself about anybody she met was what they needed most. And the second question was what she could do to satisfy that need. I'm quoting you – badly. That's what you wrote me when she died. I can't remember the way you put it exactly, but that's what you said."

"Is that what I wrote? Yes, I remember now. She was a beautiful woman. I had never met anybody like her before. For a while I was quite bewildered that anybody like her could cherish you for being what you were instead of what they had decided you ought to be. I wish I had been able to know her better."

They stretched out in the Berbice chairs for a little longer, their heels on the parapet of the verandah, finished the brandy, and talking only as it came to them while the city below grew a rash of dark patches. Then, because neither had slept very much since early the previous morning, they went to their beds.

But neither could sleep. And lying awake in the room which had been hers since she could remember, Deborah heard her half-brother open the door of the guest room across the corridor and go down to the pantry where the ring of house keys was kept on a hook screwed into the wall. She lay listening as he opened the door onto the verandah; and after a while she got up too, put on her housecoat and slippers and went through the dark house into the milky radiance of the moonlit verandah, down the driveway and across the lawn to where David had turned on the lights in the study that their father had built under the flame of the forest.

He was sitting on the little iron cot under the window that overlooked the valley, with his chin in his hands and his elbows on his knees.

"Hi," she said from the doorway, and came into the study and pulled the old, high-backed mahogany Windsor chair round from the roll-top desk and sat down. "You too?" she asked him.

He nodded between his hands.

"I was getting wider and wider awake by the minute. And yet I'm bloody tired. Exhausted. This last picture has been a brute. Or perhaps I haven't got what I once had. I used to be able to outlast anybody on location, even the youngest grips, *and* then sit up half the night running what we'd shot during the day, blocking out scene changes, sometimes working out a whole new scene. But now . . ." He shook his head, and in the totalitarian glare from the fluorescent tube in the centre of the ceiling she could see how much the colour had faded from the sandy hair since his last visit. She had not noticed it when they met at the airport because of the false vividness several weeks of Bahamas sun had given to the thin skin, but she could see it now. Even the pale eyes behind the nearly colourless lashes seemed to have become diluted.

"Poor old thing," she said, teasing him so he might not catch the pity in her voice. "All washed up at forty-five, like an athlete. Go on with you. You're tired, but then you always are towards the end of a picture. What was the name of that nice man you brought to see us that time? You know, after you'd done that job in America and somebody lent you that enormous house outside New Bay for the summer. What *was* his name? Ian? Colin? He was in films too."

"You mean Neill?" he asked. "Neill Bruce? He's still very much in films although we haven't worked together lately. He's about the best thing behind the camera since Griffith, but the public never registers a camera-man. Why, what does he have to do with my being tired?"

"Nothing, really. I only meant that he told me one day when you'd come over to see us that you used up more of yourself in every picture than any other director he'd ever worked with. He said that's why everybody loved working with you. That you became everybody on the set in turn and saw the whole thing through their eyes."

"That's what I call the Brueghel effect." He smiled briefly at her, with great fondness, but from far away. "You must have seen his *Fall of Icarus,* with the peasant ploughing and taking up the whole foreground – the whole of the picture, really – and Icarus just a tiny, unnoticed splash in a hazy sea far far off in the background. That's what a director has to try to do: to realize that every picture is a happening with as many centres of observation as there are people in it."

He got up and came over to where she sat, his hands in the pockets of his dressing gown, and smiled again. Then he turned and went over to the wall facing the foot of the cot on which he had been sitting. Like the other walls, the one before which he now stood was shelved, on every surface without a window, from floor to ceiling with unstained pitchpine planks laid across right-angled aluminium brackets, each shelf crammed with books. From where he stood, she knew he was looking at the books their father had written.

"He had a thing about his own books," she said. "He would only keep one copy of each on the shelves in here, along with a copy of the American edition, of course, and one from each translation."

"I know," he said. "He told me that once. He said it felt like cheating to have more than one copy from any one country on show." He was moving his forefinger along the copies of the books their father had written, his lips moving as he tallied, and now he asked her, "Why did you bring up Neill Bruce just now?"

"Why? What d'you mean? I told you. Because of what he said about you. To try and give you a boost. He – "

"There's nothing I can do about that bit of me, you know. I mean, there's not likely to be any sudden conversion of taste, even supposing I want to be converted."

"*David!* You idiot. Stop it! Who you fuck is your business, for God's sake. Honestly, darling. I wasn't even thinking of anything else when I mentioned Neill Bruce. I was only remembering how he'd spoken about you. As a pro he respected. And how proud I was that the other one of the two men closest to me had got that sort of respect too. I honestly, truly, couldn't remember Neill's name when I asked you. I could only remember what he'd said." She leaned forward and grinned at him with carefully fashioned casualness. "You're an old booby, aren't you?" she said. "So you like men, and I like men. Christ, brother dear, that gives us one more thing in common. D'you think I love you any less because of *that?*"

"I mean," he said heavily, "that it doesn't seem as though there are going to be any more Renfrews. You've got a different name and joined a different family now. And it wouldn't really be fair for me to try to pass the name on, would it? That would be a pretty squalid thing to do. All he's got left apart from us two are these." He brushed the backs of his nails along the spines of the books he had been counting.

She got up then and went across to him, knowing that on what she said and did in the next minute, a man's use and perhaps his life depended. She had never been asked to do something like this before, and when she realized what would happen to another if she failed she knew that what had still been very young and careless and easy in her had gone out of her and that she would never have it again.

"David," she said and wrapped her arms around his neck, leaning her greater weight and height on him so he was forced to hold her to keep his balance, "dear, sweet old brother David. I don't think I could have kept up like this if you hadn't been able to come. Tomorrow is going to be pretty bad. I know it. I'm going to need you so badly then."

"I'll be here," he said. "Don't worry. I'll be here as long as you need me."

"Come on, now," she told him. "Let's go up and have a drink. We didn't have enough, that's why we can't sleep. There's no brandy left but there's plenty of whisky. When you think I've had enough, or when you've had enough, just say so and we'll call it a night. But I need you to talk to, David, and to be with. If you hadn't been able to come, I don't know what I'd have done."

He held her closer and said, "Go on up. I'll be right behind you, I promise. I'll be up before you've got the drinks ready."

He watched her go from the study, down the steps and across the lawn to the driveway, the swirling, brilliant pattern of her short housecoat, her bright hair and the glossily tanned skin of her legs all bleached in the flooding moonlight.

When she turned the steep corner that led to the front of the house, he walked slowly over to the light switch by the door, not looking back at the books nor at the old-fashioned, high-walled roll-top desk into which death had thrust Martin Renfrew.

He switched off the light and from the step drew the door shut and locked it. He went down the three shallow steps and walked across the lawn to the gate. The dew on the coarse grass was pleasantly cool through the thin leather of his slippers.

At the gate he stood for a little longer than he had told Deborah he would be, looking down the winding hill road. The black asphalt was ash-grey under the moon until it curved into darkness out of sight, through the shadows of the two huge yoke trees that had been there when he was first driven up the road twenty-two years before.

Then he turned and began to walk up the driveway to where a headlong small child, ecstatically squealing its first triumph over dangerous courses, tumbled from the arms of a laughing woman into his.

Appendix: From a Journal

1954. April 24th. Newhaven.

The quite unbelievable selfishness of Paris: an ugly, terrible concentration on the brute fact of staying alive. The people remind me of men struggling perpetually in a quicksand, where they can only keep from suffocation by the most intricate, unflagging effort. It is a callousness born of mortal fear, and it is more marked among the artists than any other group. Everyone understands that if he were to pause for an instant and consider another it might be his death. This, and the wandering groups of beggars, the hunched, boneless sacks of rags you see crumpled against the wall of every Metro corridor; sunk in a sleep that is not really recuperation, but the bottom point of destitution.

That's the bad side of Paris. And the good? The intelligence, the seriousness with which this city seems to endow everyone who comes to it. There is the trivial and the second-rate too, of course, but the people in Paris are readier to accept the prime and adventurous explorations in art than in any other city I have seen. They take experiment and originality for granted. This is the good thing about Paris. This, and the manner in which it very firmly insists on elegance in the design of the city and quality in the food and drink. Nothing in Paris, not even the Eiffel Tower, can quite escape a little element of fineness: there is nothing there quite as grossly dead as the Albert Memorial. Nothing that asphyxiates you so completely with its corruption as Regent Street.

September 5th. Chateauneuf.

The house with green shutters: the home of Madame T. and her four ripe, handsome daughters. A tall, blank-faced building that overhangs the road like a cliff. The three rows of green shutters are always closed. A long double flight of stairs leads up from the yard to the entrance on the first floor. Over the doorway is a vine, and in the shadow of the stairs before the house, a little white rabbit in a cage.

No man ever seems to call at the house. Often when I pass, the eldest of the daughters is sitting on one of the long flights of steps, sunning the taut glossy skin of her full legs, with her dress pulled up to the waist. Her sisters and two or three young girl cousins are either in the yard or leaning out of the kitchen window. Madame T., large, smiling, and fertile, beams from the landing. Everywhere the female seems to be spilling out of the shuttered recesses of this house. But never a single man. Never a lover, a would-be lover, a caller. Where, I ask myself, are the men in their lives? And sometimes, less idly, what has happened to them?

September 20th. Chateauneuf.

Autumn is perhaps the really great season. Great in the sense of a majestic serenity, a calm and ordered music that no other season can show. Now the roof of the sky at night is higher, smoother and clearer than any other sky I can remember. The air seems stiller and more delicious in temperature. Even the crickets have lost that insistent raucousness of summer and play a deliberate, melodious counterpoint.

During the days, the blue is inconceivably deep and pure and I seem to be seeing the line of pines on the hill, against the sky, for the first time. Everywhere, in the fields and on the hills, the colours have become softer, richer, more subtle. The whole land breathes a reassuring benevolence and plenty, and the houses are received more closely into the landscape; they don't stand so starkly against it as they did a month ago. Everywhere, during the days now, there is a spilling of transparent gold, blue and green.

October 26th. London.

England for me, now, has become more than a place where I live because of certain national advantages. It seems to have seized me at a physical and emotional level which I can't yet wholly explain. My sensuous appreciation, for instance, which in Paris is almost abstract (a cold appreciation of form in which women, houses, customs are all part of an aesthetic pattern), in London is immediately more personal, more painful, closer related to my creative urge. Particularly so in my relationships to women: in Paris I feel almost no sexual desire – at the most a casual hurry of dry lust – come and gone like a powder of fine spray in the face. Utterly different to the slow, powerful tides of desire and appreciation that stir in me when I go about in London.

Walking in London today, over Westminster Bridge, my delight in the sight, smell, and feel of the purple-grey mist, the dirty water, the crowds; my relish of speech rhythms and the sound of London – all this sensed with the intensity of a convalescent.

The middle twenties is probably the most egotistical age. A man is old enough then to consciously order his powers and to have a good idea of the function his powers can play in the world. But he is also young enough to be frightened of those powers being obscured by a jealous conspiracy of elders: particularly those elders who are his friends.

Not yet old enough to accept the biological relationship of the older and younger generation, he often works out all his resentment and anxiety on one particular member of the former. This hostility is intensified by the fact that in his relationship with older men he still has a residue of the childish sense of obligation: vestigial traces of that uneasy sense of being actually or potentially a malefactor, which is a concept of themselves adults carefully build into children as a means of protecting the grown-up world. The resentment that a man of twenty-five feels on sensing, in himself, this disadvantage of childhood can make his hostility – to the older person he selects as the symbol of his dependence – ungovernable, and ferociously bitter. It enters even his dreams.

November 5th. London.

"I am glad to think that my youth is past and it never can return – that time of disappointed experience when a man possesses nothing, not even himself." (Florence Nightingale to her father in 1852.)

Of the thirteen years between seventeen and thirty, it's only the first three or four which give any pleasure to a man of imagination. Those are the years when the strict conventions, the stiff tribal inhibitions of childhood are abandoned. And this coincides with the eager tumbling rush of golden physical energy which is quite inexhaustible and which meets every experience with the confidence of a puppy and the heat of a passionate virgin.

But the between years! When you no longer have the quite fantastic endowments of youth and that formidable, marvellous energy which flings you into life and sanctifies, somehow, every mistake, every awkwardness. Those between years, the twenties, they're the time when you know less than you ever have or will. When you fear more. When you can excuse yourself for nothing. You have all the equipment you're ever likely to have and your mistakes are all because you haven't taken the trouble to learn the use of it. You have no high cards to play from: as children have honesty, and young people have their magnificent energies. All you have, and what helps you to survive, is a capacity for not breaking, for withdrawing in order to digest the jagged, bewildering, leaden mass. At thirty, the teeth worn to the irreducible stubs, the body scarred to the point where there is no surface tissue left to bleed, at thirty you've learnt a habit of acceptance and a habit of catching yourself in your characteristic ugliness. This sort of makeshift honesty generates an energy that's not as flexible or tumultuous as that of the teens but surer of what it can do and where it wants to go.

1955. March 9th. London.

The thing every writer goes for is the thing no writer ever gets. It's the thing the big painters achieve. To catch, in one face, one cup, one apple, one woman's dress, all the tears and love, all the wine and craft, all the fertility, all the complexity of human invention that ever was.

September 6th. London.

Went to the Festival Hall last night for the Beethoven concert. Finale of the Seventh done magnificently by Norman Mar and the London Symphony; but the Scherzo and Trio of the third movement, at one time my favourite moment in all music, lacked clarity in the dividing line. It is absolutely necessary to have the transitions so precisely managed that they shock. Otherwise the whole direction of this movement becomes uncertain.

March 15th. Off Barbados.

The little Venezuelan stowaway: he's about fifteen or sixteen; the real mulatto type; dark, rich, chocolaty skin, strong hair closely shaved on a broad-based, narrowing, bullet skull; a face as round and firm as a cannon ball; a short, blunt nose and small feminine mouth; a stocky, packed body dressed in two cast-off vests and an old pair of sailor's pants which, rolled up to their knees, still hang just above his ankles. He has seen fifteen countries since he stowed away and enjoys a protected, cat's sort of existence aboard by playing a calculated, skilful role between court jester and village idiot.

March 18th. Off Curaçao.

Campo Alegre. Two wide, open, barn-like bars, blistered and drab. Two jukeboxes, one of them taller than a tall man. The girls come from all over the Caribbean and are allowed to stay a month. They have their cabins in rows around the two bars. Each cabin has one almost furnitureless entrance room, with a concrete floor and no wallpaper, and a hot, dark little bedroom with a low narrow bed and a small bedside table. The girls dress mostly in matador pants and bright blouses but only a few of them look very attractive. The black women mostly. Across the road from the compound is a thick grove of manchineel trees.

1957. July 25th. Antigua.

The parched, enormous basin of a valley, and the hot blue sea biting into it as you come down from Shirley Heights. I have never seen anything as brittle-looking and dry as the valley on the other side of the hill from English Harbour. So dry that the smoke from a burning field in the middle of it, and the charred, black earth seemed natural and unsurprising, as if the flames had started spontaneously.

Interviewed old M.S.[1] this afternoon. He is intelligent, astute and has made money. Yet there is something pathetic about him. Something puzzled and lost. He was given a set of reactions and beliefs and without warning they were challenged (and successfully challenged) while he was not even properly aware of defiance being prepared. Now he finds that there is a whole territory – territories? – of life that he cannot accept; he feels awkward, out of harmony with the new men and the new situations. And half of his resentment and disgust springs from the fact that he is too intelligent not to realize that his innate gifts have missed the boat because he equated his prejudices with an unchangeable pattern of society.

An interesting contrast to R.H.,[2] who is also in opposition but fighting, substantially, on the same ground; who uses naturally the same terms of reference as his opponents; who is, in fact, one of the new men produced by the new situation. R.H. has confidence; M.S. is petulant.

August 16th. Georgetown, British Guiana.

Before the courthouse last week, when it looked as if Balram Singh Rai would win, the old woman was saying bitterly: "We race build them up and now dey pull we race down."

All part of the strange, depressing paralysis that seems to shackle the energies of the African in British Guiana. A truly dispossessed person who made one enormous pioneer effort under the whip and has refused to encounter the equal torment of free labour since. Slowly but visibly his

---

1. Possibly Alexander Moody-Stuart, "the recognized leader of the plantocracy and the ruling class", who had been managing director of Antigua Syndicate Estates Ltd and a member of the legislature and executive council. Robert J. Alexander, with Eldon M. Parker, *A History of Organized Labor in the English-speaking West Indies* (Westport, CT: Praeger, 2004), 158.

2. Possibly Antiguan politician Robert Hall (1909–1994), also a white planter and farmer. https://en.wikipedia.org/wiki/Robert_Hall_(Antiguan_politician)

energy is bleeding away because he refuses to recognize that the only reference possible from him to an environment is to Guiana. Because he will not accept the incomparable challenge of having to find his naked soul, and having found that to clothe it with the heritage and myth of an entire world. He came here naked and nothing or no one can ever replace what he had to leave. The one people who had to be adult from birth.

The anguish of such a life has filled him with terror and a desperate need to find a matrix. A search in which he will be everlastingly disappointed, until he finds the womb in himself, in his integral core.

In Guiana he has not so much been conscious of his race as of his lack of it. Unlike the East Indians who feel that in their folk they have all they need and who have accepted the challenge of the land and increase the territory of the folk.

The pathetic, despicable nostalgia for a past that corrupts so many Negroes like N. The retreat into apologia for their condition, their endless "historical" explanations and their lack of any direction. The sentimental camaraderie of skin which provides the cheap thrill of being "African". Pitiful in its implications of future slavery.

The Indian knows what he wants. He knows it ten yards at a time inland from the coast.

Perhaps the most solid achievement of the Jamaican people up to now is the way they have divested themselves of nostalgia; the way in which they have accepted the nakedness of their condition and attempt to clothe it without fear of losing integrity.

I could not help feeling that the Marcus Garvey statue was, even for the illiterate, more a realistic recognition of expedient political service than a masturbatory orgy of sentimental nostalgia.

The Indian barman told me: "Boss, our party in now. Ten years from now we buy niggers for two dollars apiece. God give all race dem special sickness. De Indian man have cough; de Portugee have big foot; but de nigger – God mek he lazy an' dat is incurable."

July 25th. Amboise.

Why is medieval architecture so loaded with meaning?[3] We can despise the monotony, the insularity, the rigid cage and strict pattern which engulfed the individual life of the Middle Ages, and yet – we come suddenly on a column or corner or leap of stone that is so shattering, so enormous in implication that we are humiliated. It cannot be contained cerebrally; as even the greatest Renaissance architecture can be understood, or, more properly, reduced. There is, always, even in the profane great building of the Middle Ages something just beyond our rational grasp; some perception or understanding or intimate life – knowledge that makes it luminous with assurance, strengthens it immeasurably, with a phenomenal certitude. One's instinctive, first response to a supreme example of the medieval structure is an astonished, great "Oh!" Faced suddenly with the Renaissance in full splendour, one is aware of a delightful wrench as the intellect is extended – but extended within conceivable limits.

July 26th. Pierre Bufliere (Haute-Vienne).

Trying to define, precisely, all the changes in structure, shape, colour as we have passed from Normandy into Ile de France, into La Beauce, the Touraine and Limousin. It is most important for a novelist that he learn to reduce a landscape –and sometimes the figures in it – to essentials. That is one of the things the writer learns from the great painters. One of the most important things: capturing a landscape, an environment with fidelity, selecting so that always this is how the sky was, and the light on the horizon, and the most important colours on the most important contours, and, above all, the large, dominant single detail in the foreground – man,

---

3. Château at Amboise was actually begun in the Middle Ages but expanded and remodelled during the Renaissance when it was a favoured royal residence. My thanks to Fragano Ledgister (personal communication, 16 August 2016) for this observation.

beast or bower – which gives unity to what you have "impressed" on the reader, which focuses the environment. To get it all, truly, you have to watch closely all the time, close your eyes every now and again for a tenth of a second and reproduce exactly on your inner plates, the exact line of march that a stand of oak makes across the crest of a field, the exact colour that is caught in a deep fold between the red of a roof and the tawny dark of nearly ripe wheat, the way that stacked corn is a dry lion colour on the top side but shadowed grey underneath, the curious effortless glide a family has as they walk in single file through a wheat field, with the father waist high and the smallest child only a hat and a brown-pink face in the tall grass.

All this must be learnt, equally with learning people. It is the salt to all the food a writer eats.

August 5th. Bolzano-Merano.

The valley and the plain are the two great matrices of anything worth keeping in Europe. The hill and mountain country produce interesting but essentially marginal examples: by-products of the main stems.

We have had no plateau cultures in Europe as in Asia or America.

September 17th. Midhurst.

The writer must hold himself in readiness for the moments when he meets himself descending the stairway: that odd, bemused half-stranger, ready to hurry past you with a cocked glance full of truculence and anxiety, disturbed because he has met you before and does not remember when, or whether he liked you or not. He is the visitor from the future (and how? How did he get before you on the stairway?), not capable of anything until you seize him and make an ascent – he for the second time.

October 9th.

The greatest novelist is only the tomb of a poet sacrificed.

1959. January 29th.

The writer is such a monstrous creature that he has to be very good indeed if society is to forgive him. The fond, patronizing indulgence – or symbolic portent – with which other failures are regarded (*vide* the "whisky priest", the third-rate music-hall artist, even the suicide, and so on) is never the lot of the bad writer. All the odium and terror which people instinctively feel for this profession is paid off in the bored contempt with which they treat the unfortunate man of words who never quite comes up to scratch.

Perhaps the residue of archaic wisdom which tells them that other failures are the failures of personality, whereas a writer, even the worst, has no personality to ruin. All that makes him a person has been wound off, like a snake's skin, onto the frame of his work. Words are the only instruments that perform this consistent mutilation. Paint, music, stone, the stage, all enrich rather than diminish the agents who operate in them.

Acknowledgements

My thanks to Linda Van Ierssel, dear friend and trusted colleague: without her professional and personal encouragement, this collection would have remained a good intention. I am particularly happy that these stories have found their home at the University of the West Indies Press because the university itself was a home of sorts to my father, who was a lecturer and later resident tutor at the university's Creative Arts Centre (now the Philip Sherlock Centre for the Creative Arts) and a fixture of the Mona campus, in his Panama hat and with cigarette in hand, for many years.

I am grateful beyond measure to Kim Robinson-Walcott and Marlon James for their excellent contributions to this collection. Thanks also to Rachel Mordecai, Fragano Ledgister, Franklin Knight and Anthony Maingot for answering questions along the way; to Natalya Rattan, archivist at the Thomas Fisher Rare Book Library, University of Toronto, for assistance with the *Tamarack Review*; to Lisa Samuel, Jean D'Costa, Alex Sosa and Lynn Henry for being good listeners; to Judy Raymond for her careful proofreading; and to Robert Harris for his design. And thanks to Kevin Kelly for that which cannot be quantified or labelled.

CPSIA information can be obtained
at www.ICGtesting.com
Printed in the USA
LVOW08s0958291216
PP11769700001B/3/P